KING
OF THE
ROADKILLS

KING OF THE ROADKILLS

BUCKY SINISTER

MANIC D PRESS
SAN FRANCISCO

Cover art by Frank Kozik   Cover design by Scott Idleman/BLINK
                       Comix artwork by Chuck Sperry

Earlier versions of some of these pieces originally appeared in *Signs of Life, 12 Bowls of Glass, Asphalt Rivers, A Friend and A Killer, Symphony of the Damned*, and *Last Gasp Comix and Stories #1 & 2*.

The publisher wishes to thank Jon Longhi, Ron Turner, Frank Kozik, Last Gasp, and Martin Sprouse.

Library of Congress Cataloging-in-Publication Data

Sinister, Bucky, 1969-
    King of the roadkills / Bucky Sinister.
       p.   cm.
    ISBN 0-916397-37-8 (paperback)
    1. Punk culture--United States--Literary collections.   2. Science
fiction, American.   I. Title.
PS3569.I5757K56 1995
813'.54--dc20
                                                          95-2046
                                                          CIP

Distributed by Publishers Group West

CONTENTS

Dedicated to the music and members of
Steel Pole Bathtub
their live shows and recordings have been the biggest of inspirations

KING OF THE ROADKILLS

WHEN THEY ASKED MOTHER WHAT WAS FOR DINNER, SHE SAID, "SEX, DRUGS, AND JESUS CHRIST," AND THEY SAID, "AGAIN?"

Who slashed the tires on the American Dream? Once again the car is not where I left it. The hubcaps have been stolen and the pinstripes have been made into UPC bar codes. Somewhere in the universe a radio is playing the national anthem with no speakers. I am tired of looking around the neighborhood for something with the keys in it. Either the government should park my car or I should learn to hot wire.

The zombies said no to my magic mushrooms. I thought they'd be partial to fungus but I had them all wrong. They were speed freaks and they weren't into the blind man's bluff trip with their hands. They cut hedges and washed cars and each had their own mausoleum and funeral plot. They didn't seem to care that the mausoleums only came in five flavors. There were millions of them sleepwalking through some dream they called America.

She tried to drive the American Dream across the country but the transmission fell out on a hill in San Francisco. She could not get the car fixed and she did not fall in love so she went back home to the Midwest. Now she takes drugs to keep up with the insanity of her family and the last time I saw her she was trying to bang her head on the floor but I wouldn't let her.

We are the dairy products left out of the American Dream and we have been blamed for going bad. Anxiety disorders grow on us like mold. But despite my lumps and curds I stagger on through the rusted swing sets and the twenty-four-hour restaurants, being careful of the zombies, for I have heard you should never wake up anyone who is sleepwalking.

TWO-TENTHS OF AN ENTIRE SECOND

"Can't get good speed anymore," they complained. "It's all cut with acid now."

The one who wasn't listening asked the sun to come up and it said, "No."

"Hey, everybody," the inattentive one said. "The sun has refused to come up." The others were quite shocked at the news, and they immediately stopped their conversation for two-tenths of an entire second. For a while all you could hear was the sound of brain cells popping.

Then someone said, "Let's form a committee." Someone else said, "Good idea," and someone else took credit for it. Meanwhile, the someone who talked to the sun got bored and started talking to the sun again.

Now the sun knows just about everything that the moon don't know so it was asked to grant an answer to a question. Another thing about the sun: it never lies. The question was, "Who killed Kennedy?" and the sun replied, "Which one?" and refused to answer any more questions.

The sun can be a real smartass when it wants to be.

BEER CITY

There is a city in the United States whose main product is beer. The beer company employs most of the locals, and when these people get off work they go to see the pro baseball team, owned by the company, that plays in the company-owned stadium, and they consume beer products they have spent all day packaging.

One day in the Dominican Republic, a young man named Jose, with a good arm, found a boat called the American Dream and sailed for Beer City. He pitched for the Beer City baseball team and soon he was sending enough money home to support his entire extended family. Jose hated beer, and he didn't even like baseball that much, but the money was good and his family was happy.

The rally song for the Beer City baseball team was the jingle for the beer commercial. Before every crucial pitch, the pipe organ would start up with the jingle and the crowd would clap along. Jose came to associate the jingle with high stress.

Jose didn't speak English. The only one on the whole team who spoke any Spanish was the pitching coach, and he only knew baseball words. Jose was lonely and stressed out, so he would take walks around the city at night to try to calm down. But the people of Beer City started looking fatter, paler, and pasty. They drooled and oozed a foamy substance. By the all-star break, everyone looked like albino frogs and smelled rancid.

Jose longed for away games, but even then, alone in his hotel room watching TV, the beer commercial would come on, the jingle would play. The walls would breathe a little bit deeper, and the colors would glow a little bit more.

Jose became one of the greatest pitchers of all time with all his adrenaline flowing during a game. But in the final game of the World Series, he struck out the last batter by throwing the ball straight into the mouth of a seven-headed, fire-breathing Clydesdale. The screaming team rushed up to the mound and hugged him, the jingle started up, and someone poured beer on his head. Then Jose started hollering and the doctors are still trying to get him to stop.

Jose, can you see, by the dreams' early light, Jackie Robinson swinging from the scoreboard? Did you hear somebody slid into the American Dream and spiked it with six-inch cleats? It never really healed and was traded for a state of consciousness to be named later.

THAT SPECIAL LOOK

Kathy looked into her coffee. Mark looked at Kathy. Laundry, spinning in dryers, looked at them.

Mark removed himself from the bar and sat at Kathy's table. Kathy closed her eyes and wished him away, but it didn't work.

"Hi, mind if I sit with you?" Mark said. He looked at Kathy.

"You're already sitting with me," Kathy said. She looked into her spoon. The spoon curved her reflection and gave it back to her.

Kathy looked at anything but Mark. Mark looked at Kathy. The tables, chairs, napkin dispensers, and the ashtrays wished they didn't have to keep watching this same scene over and over.

Kathy just wanted to be left alone. Most of her life she had been alone, and eventually it bothered her. When she finally was not alone any longer, Kathy realized it was the only way she could survive. Now she was alone again and she never wanted it to change.

Mark just wanted someone in his life. He wanted a touch. He wanted a laugh. He wanted a grasp at being in love. He had a fear of dying alone.

"I saw you at my performance last night," Mark said. He actually had seen her, although he used this line on many women.

"I work at that club. I was paid to be there," Kathy said. She wanted to sound like she hadn't enjoyed it and Mark took it that way, but Kathy had seen him other places and had two of his books and one of his albums at home. She liked his work but she didn't want to talk to him.

Kathy looked at the ashtray. Mark looked at Kathy. A homeless man looked through the window at Mark's cigarette.

"Look, why do you come here if you don't want to talk to me? This is the hottest social spot in the city," Mark said. People were easy for him to pick up here, especially when they found out who he was.

"I live practically next door. It's the closest laundromat around. I don't care if it has a full bar or not," Kathy said. She decided never to read his books again. She decided never to listen to his album again. She wanted his words to stop. She just wanted to be left alone.

Kathy looked at the signs on the wall. Mark looked at Kathy. The phone started to ring.

"But what's your problem? I mean, I'm a good-looking popular healthy guy and I just want to get to know you, okay? I just want someone to talk to. I just want a friend. What is your problem?" Mark said. When he was ten years old, he was at the circus and saw an acrobat miss the trapeze. The acrobat clawed the air with the same desperation Mark was now feeling.

Kathy couldn't explain her problem. She just saw it as the way things were, not as a problem. She just wanted to be left alone. She closed her eyes and wished him away. This time, it worked.

"Mark, it's your agent on the phone," the bartender said. Mark got up to take the call. When Kathy opened her eyes, he was no longer sitting with her.

"Nice talking with you. Maybe I'll see you again," Mark said, hanging up the phone. He went out the door. The homeless man stabbed him in the alley by his car. Mark looked up from a circus floor and bled to death.

Kathy realized her laundry was done drying. She put it in a bag and went home, feeling relieved.

12 BOWLS OF GLASS

When the lightbulb I am changing
slips through my fingers
and explodes in the sink

like a dream I once had for myself
that was shattered the same way by reality

I turn on the faucet
and watch the water take the tiny frozen spasms of glass
down the steel throat of the sink
because I want the sink to feel like I do.

They say that you have to eat twelve bowls of the leading brand cereal
to get the nutrition you get from one bowl of Total
and maybe you have to eat twelve bowls of glass
to feel what you get from one bowl of life.

It's a wonder we all aren't screaming
like madmen in our sleep.

TIPPER GORE, ARE YOU GOING TO BAN MY KITCHEN?

if my faucet dripped backwards
I wonder if I could hear
satanic messages

and since I am used to sleeping
with hair in my face
when cockroaches crawl across my face
in the night
I do not feel it
or wake up

and I fear one night
they will form a pentagram
and dance around my bed
to the Gehenna-drumbeats
of water droplets.

THE NATURE OF OUR RELATIONSHIP

The reason we never worked out
was due to the nature of our relationship.

I could equate it to a deer
looking into the headlights
of an oncoming Buick.

We gazed at one another in fascination
blind to impending disaster
if we had stayed together
we would have been another roadkill.

But what I never have decided is
who was the deer and
who was the Buick?

TRYING TO FORGET

There are things I try so hard to forget
but forgetting them
would be like forgetting
that I have arms and legs.

And when it all gets to be too much
my body is tired
(even though I never want to sleep again)
and my eyeballs feel as if they have gone stale
and I think to myself,
"God, help me
I'm dying in here
I'm dying in my own mind."

I look around at the young professionals
waiting to go home
crowding the subways
and I think,
"Don't they know?
Can't they smell me dying in here?"

Maybe they do not know the smell of death
or maybe they cannot smell me over their own smell
of sweat and fax machines;

But I am not familiar with the smell of death either
I assume it smells something like maggots
but maybe it smells like fax machines.

I saw a girl get into a car on Geary and Leavenworth
and unlike the other girls on the street
she looked nervous

as if it were her first time to turn a trick
and I feel as nervous as she.
When I was a child, I believed in magic
and I thought everything was magic like
a litter of puppies
or a plate of warm cookies
but the first time I saw a magician
my parents told me there was no such thing as magic
and that it was all a trick
and now I know everything is a trick
but I do not know
how to turn any of them.

"A good magician never reveals his secrets,"
or so people tell me
and so far they are right.
No one has told me anything
but I have not figured anything out for myself.

If anyone knows the tricks of forgetting
whether you be a magician or a prostitute
send me the secrets of how to turn them
even if you have to fax them to me.

ALONE

You get so alone sometimes
you would catch a cockroach
put it in a bottle that you emptied by yourself
name it Mickey
and talk to it for a few days until it dies.

You get so alone sometimes
you would call someone if you knew anyone
but you don't
so you change the message on your
virgin answering machine
that you have only to make you feel like you need one.

You get so alone sometimes
that the sounds of traffic from the window
the faucet dripping
the guy upstairs moving his furniture again
and the light dribbling of your head
bumping the wall behind you as you sit on the floor
all turns into words
and you feel like the snags in the carpet and
the crack in the window
are talking to you
and you open the refrigerator
just to see the light turn on
and all the food is quiet
like they quit talking when you opened the door
and wait until you shut it to start talking again.

You get so alone sometimes
you feel like throwing all the mirrors
out your four story window

but it's the only person who ever seems to visit.
You get so alone sometimes
you sit in the corner in the same clothes
you've been wearing for three days straight
making shadow pictures on the wall
singing songs you barely know off key
making up most of the words.

You get so alone sometimes
you don't mind the way you smell
which isn't bad
compared to the rest of the apartment.

You get so alone sometimes
when you see two people talking together
you wonder what it feels like
and you want to stop thinking the same thoughts
over and over
and you start to have conversations that happened years ago
again in your head—
but this time you say the right thing.

You get so alone sometimes
that when you come to this coffeehouse
you are by yourself
and I am by myself
and you want to sit with me
and I want you to sit with me
but we sit apart and keep our mouths shut
and pretend that we want this time to ourselves
as we read a book, a paper, or write in our journals
because you get so alone sometimes
you don't think of things being
any other way.

BLEEDING FOR THE LATE NIGHT BUS

Sometime after one a.m.
while waiting for the Fillmore bus
the only other person around
was a girl in her late twenties
who asked me for a quarter.

She looked like she needed it but all I had
was twenty-one cents
so I offered that to her
which she gratefully accepted and said
"I sure wish you could come over to my place.
It's only a five-dollar thang.
What do you say?"

And even though I had five dollars
I told her I couldn't do that tonight
and she walked off
down the unburdened sidewalk
as I sat on the curb.

The concrete only got louder
with emptiness
and I watched time crawl down the street
like a Salvador Dali clock
painted with snails

and I could've been bleeding to death
and I wouldn't have known the difference.

The bus finally came
but in some ways I feel that it never has

and I feel like a bloodless zombie with five dollars
guarding the empty spots of the world
making sure
someone is around to hear it exist
although there are no trees where I live anyway.

VENICE BEACH STRAYS

Eleven-thirty at night
at a pay phone on the beach
I watched several stray dogs fight over something
only dogs would understand.

Only twenty feet away
a stray human slept beneath a palm tree.

A police patrol car came by
and the police said,
"THE BEACH IS CLOSED.
NO SLEEPING ON THE BEACH."

The beach did not look closed to me.
No one had even turned off the waves.

An unmarked but obvious police car
with a *Dare to Keep Kids Off Drugs* bumper sticker
pulled up for assistance
as a cop got out of the first car
woke up the stray human,
and made him leave
but the dogs
who were watching from a cautious distance
got to stay
and they figured it was something
only humans would understand.

THE BLACK WIDOW AND THE TRAVELING BUTCHER

"I can't believe you're serious about wanting to become a warlock," I said, trying not to laugh at Mark as he squirmed in the passenger seat.

"Take this next exit," he murmured, looking out the window.

I kept glancing at him as I drove, often as I could, but he never looked at me; he just kept staring out the window, embarrassment reeking from him like rotten eggs thrown at a house on Halloween. Since I started working with him a few months ago, I had seen him take the brunt of most of the practical jokes played in the warehouse. He always reacted badly, but he had never appeared so self-conscious before. I didn't want to make him feel worse, but I just couldn't believe he could be serious about learning black magic. I wouldn't have bothered driving him so far out of the city, but he reminded me of my runty little brother and my sentimental side, small but persuasive, made me do it.

"So just who's this lady I'm taking you to see about apprenticeship?" I said, trying to make him feel more at ease.

"Her given name is Ursula Navarre," he sighed, as if he thought I would never take him seriously. "But she goes by the name of Black Widow."

"Oooooeeeeeewooooo!" I wailed in horror movie soundtrack fashion. "Let me guess," I laughed, "she mates and kills, right?"

"Yes, she does," he said in a "so-there" type way. "Only she's never been caught. She sings about it on all her albums."

"Waitwaitwaitwait. Is this that Death Rocker lady who went to court several years ago on murder charges?"

"Yeah, that's her," he said, looking back out the window.

I started to laugh so hard I almost missed the exit. "Her! Her? You're going to try to learn real magic from her? She never killed anyone, the case was thrown out because it looked like a publicity stunt! All that witchy-poo stuff is a stage image!"

"Take a left," he mumbled, "and then go up the driveway on the right."

"I can't believe this! That's like trying to learn to talk from Mr. Ed! At least if you're going to do this you should do it right!"

I went up the driveway; it was so long that the house wasn't visible at first. Soon a two-story Colonial-style house seemed to rise from the ground at the end. The only house we could see from the driveway was hers; the surrounding forest cut off views to any neighboring estates.

"This babe must be loaded," I marveled in barely-above-minimum-wage jealousy.

"She's an heiress and a musical success," Mark stated as I parked the car right behind a new black Jaguar. He opened the door and got out.

"Beware, mortals, for you are near the web of the Black Widow," I said in a creepy voice, and followed Mark to the door. He was looking even more nervous than in the car.

As he knocked with the gargoyle knocker, an uncomfortable thought came to me. Didn't learning black magic require strange personal sacrifices? Hadn't, in the stories I read, witches traded their souls, beauty, children, or something to someone in order to start?

"Uh, Mark, how do you plan to pay for her services? You don't have enough money to get your car fixed."

Mark's head snapped around and jerked back. His face was bright red. I think that he was about to say something when the door opened.

A six foot six inch butler opened the door; he towered over both of us. I could hear organ music inside. A smell from what I guess was exotic incense danced its way up to my nose: something I had never smelled before. It was all too much like some bad movie.

"Yo, Lerch, we're here to see a Widow. One in black would be nice, but burgundy would do," I snickered. Mark kicked my foot.

The butler looked at me with disgust, like I was trick-or-treat candy you find hidden in your closet in July, and then took Mark and me to the basement. It was covered in deep maroon colors, the floor, the walls, the ceiling, everywhere that somber red. Candles and incense burned, giving the room a glow bright enough to see easily. Ursula Navarre was reclining on an eight-foot couch wearing a black robe. When she saw us, she grabbed a remote control and turned down the organ music on the CD player.

"One of you is Mark, correct?"

"I didn't know you were a psychic, too," I blurted. She gave me a look that was supposed to scare me. "He's Mark," I said. "My name is..."

"Please, have a seat," she interrupted. "Mr. Carruthers, you may leave us." She waved away the butler with a thin pale hand, fingers adorned with silver rings and crowned with inch-long black nails.

Mark sat in a chair next to the couch and Ursula went to get us drinks. I wondered why she didn't have the butler make them for us, but my chain of thought was broken by an open scrapbook lying on the couch.

The scrapbook was a photo album filled with newspaper clippings about Traveling Butcher slayings. Several papers for each killing.

"What's the fascination with the Traveling Butcher?" I asked.

From the bar she yelled, "What's not to be fascinated about? He's killed twenty-nine people in five years all over the U.S. and no one's got a clue as to who it is. He's on his way to becoming the most successful serial killer in recorded history. His trademark is severing and keeping various body parts, although no one seems to know why. By the way, he's due for another slaying; it's been at least four months since the last one. I can't wait."

Laughing a little, I looked over at Mark. A drop of sweat ran down his face like a convict making a prison break. I sniffed hard and I could smell him sweating through the incense. I was about to ask him what was wrong, why was he so nervous, when Ursula came back into the room.

She was wearing nothing but thigh-high leather boots and black gloves that went past her elbows. Did she know that was my biggest weakness?

She was suddenly beautiful, her body had the grace of a night wind, her green eyes were going supernova. She handed Mark and me silver chalices. I was surprised he could hold his without spilling it; I would've helped him but I was too busy bathing my eyes in her.

I took a drink, trying to calm down, feeling as if I were staring at a sidewalk from a twenty-story building ledge. The drink was some type of wine I had never had before: it dissolved on my tongue and palate to their delight, but all I could think of was her.

She sat down on my lap, facing me, straddling my legs. Her hands went around me and her black nails began scraping my back like coffin nails, and her tongue was whipping my ear. I was approaching Nirvana until my eyes clicked open suddenly like a camera shutter.

The picture I saw was Mark shaking with his head in his hands, which was the way he acted when he was breaking down from ridicule or stress. Reality hit me like a car wrapping itself around a telephone pole. I felt stupid for letting that shuck set me up and coming close to falling for it. I kept my nerve and decided to get out of this in my own infamous way.

I took my stiletto from my jacket pocket, reached around Ursula to that oh-so-effective spot on the back and hit the release button. The blade shot in, Ursula snapped her head back as if she were looking at my hairline, stuck that heavenly tongue out, gagged, and died. I expected a grisly scream or something, but that was it. Dramatic people rarely live up to their reputation when nailed to the wall.

I took the blade out and made a quick slice around her left ear, which came off easily, jammed it in my mouth, and sucked. I pushed the corpse forward and let it fall on the floor.

Mark spoke for the first time since we left the car. "Ohmygod! Ohmygod! Ohmygod!"

I spit the ear out, caught it, and put it in my pocket along with my knife.

"You know, Markie boy," I said with a bloody-tooth grin, "I bet you never would've guessed that I'm a cannibal. Even further from your mind would be that I am the Traveling Butcher. I didn't get this far leaving witnesses."

Mark's legs understood what was coming next and they bolted him to the stairway. I took my twenty-two pistol out of my other jacket pocket and shot him right between the shoulder blades. He wasn't dead, but he wasn't going anywhere.

Mark was lying facedown on the stairway, choking, when I shot him again at the base of the skull. His blood exploded out his mouth and tackily clashed against the maroon carpet. I took out my knife, cut off his fingertips, and stuffed them in my mouth like marbles.

I put my knife back, grabbed the scrapbook from the couch, and ran upstairs, hoping to get to Mr. Carruthers before he called the police.

DEVON'S DEMONDOOBIE AND THE PAISLEY BIKERS

Devon's quarter-ounce joint had all of us eagerly anticipating Methuselah's party. Devon had bought a pound of pot and had been selling to everyone for quite a while. He only sold the kind buds and was always generous to his friends. He told everyone that he had rolled one monster joint with all the shake using ten rolling papers which he would be bringing by Methuselah's party. Ron, Dennis, Bob, and myself showed up early.

Bob still had thirteen hits of acid that he bought at the Jerry Garcia shows, and since he was planning a trip to the next Dead show to score some more, he wanted to get rid of what he had. We decided that Electric Kool-Aid was the best idea.

Ron and Dennis Bardley and their quasi-brother Bob were bonafide Deadheads, but somehow they had gotten through their illustrious psychedelic careers without having actually made any electric punch, so no one knew for sure what proportions would be correct. The only container Methuselah had to make the punch in was a long-vacant fishbowl, so we poured in the hot water, dumped in the Kool-Aid, and dropped in all thirteen hits.

Anyone could have a dixie cup full, first-come, first-served, until it was gone. We drank ours, a few people came and had theirs, and things were quiet for a little while. We thought maybe no one was coming. I convinced them to let me have a second cup since I didn't smoke pot and never drank while frying on acid. I downed the second without any effect. No one's trip was coming on, and we thought it might have been too diluted.

People started arriving, and within ten minutes, the punch was gone. I still wasn't feeling anything when Julio came in.

"Hey, Iggy, homeboy," he said with whiskey breath, slapping me on the shoulder. Julio and his friend Manny had sold me my very first hit of acid about five months before. "Find Dennis and I'll dose you guys."

I was in the mood to fry, and I knew his stuff was good. I found Dennis, pulled him over to Julio, and he put the squares on our tongues.

"You guys have a good time," he said with a smile, and slipped through a crowd that had sprouted from the carpet. When I tried to follow him with my eyes, waves rolled across my vision and I almost lost my balance.

I was new to LSD, but I knew this was not from the hit I had just been given. This feeling came from the first cup of punch, and I still had quite a ways to go. A comfortable place to sit and melt away was in order. I looked around for Ron, Dennis, and Bob, but they were standing around the keg drinking beer and playing their usual mind games with anyone who walked by. I saw my friend, Rita, sitting by the futon.

"Hey, Iggy, howya doin'?" she asked.

"You had some of the punch, right?"

"Yeah, what about it?"

"Well, I had two and then Julio gave me another hit on top of all that."

At first she had the "you're kidding" disbelief look, which evolved to the "you idiot" anger look, finally stopping at the "you poor thing" pity expression.

"Iggy, you really shouldn't have done that," she scolded motherly. She took my hand and rubbed it. "Just hang out with me, I'll be your reality anchor."

People kept coming in and I kept coming on. It was a studio apartment so it was quickly packed, even with most of the crowd outside. Claustrophobia made each group of people a bit nervous. Then someone said the magic words.

"Hey, Devon's here!"

The crowd rushed outside and came back in as a writhing mob of tie-dyes and long hair spouting "Wow, man"s. Somewhere at the center was Devon and the Demondoobie from Hell. Smoke was rising up like someone had lit all the matches in a matchbook at once. One by one, the beast spewed forth a thoroughly baked messenger child. Much faster than I thought it would happen, people were talking about the roach. I would've gotten up to at least take a look, but my own drugs had me taking root in the carpet.

The Oscar Meyer Special was done with, but had accomplished its mission extremely well. The overly crowded crowd suddenly released their social inhibitions and were all friendly and talking. Julio had made many sales on top of the select few who had the punch. I was having the most intense visual experience of my acid days to that point, and Rita and I were having a good time together as Siamese twins joined at the third eye. Patterns were thrown up all over the walls, the road map of Europe became veins and pulsed the black dots into the ocean, most of the people liked the music, and everybody in general was having a good time. It was such a good time that everybody should have known to leave because things could only get worse.

This was about the time that Manny Alvarado showed up with his biker friends from Venice Beach. They were all on speed and drinking Jack Daniel's, yelling and screaming like Vikings.

About half of the people at this party were Jewish. Even though I knew of none there who observed anything more than a holiday or two, it was part of their identity. Of the Jewish people there, about half were frying. Bikers can be scary enough on their own to anybody, but these guys had swastikas, iron crosses, SS logos, and other Nazi symbols tattooed in faded colors all over their arms. Immediately, about one quarter of the party started having a bad trip, freezing into a gaped mouth terror pose.

I was peaking when Manny found me on the floor with Rita. He bent down into my face and called his friends over.

"This is my homeboy, Iggy. He's cool as fuck." Manny danced away.

A biker leaned down into my face, his nose looking to be about twice the size of the rest of his face, as the background of the room fisheyed. In a voice played at a slow RPM he said, "Heeeeyy, arrrrrre yooooouuuuu frrrrrooooom Veeeeeenice?" He flashed the hood sign for Venice and the whole picture froze up except for extremely tiny and mesmerizing paisleys. I had never in my life dreamed that paisleys were inspired by anything other than microorganisms, but they would never look the same to me again.

"No, Culver City," I found myself saying when time resumed. The biker ran away to dance with his buddies to the music they had put on: a loud, fast, probably local band. "Wow," was the only thing I could think of to say at the time.

People started leaving; they had their THC and the LSD they came for, and the scene was changing with the antics of three hogstraddlers. One was going up to every woman there with the line, "I betcha ten bucks I got your name tattooed on my dick," and when he finally whipped it out, there were the words *Your Name*. They were getting louder and drunker and even a bit scarier. This was when Rita's ride decided to go home.

"I've gotta go, my ride's leaving," she said with regret. My world started to unravel. Rita disappeared and it was just me, the bikers, and anyone else who was too blitzed to leave.

At one point, my eyes were focused on nowhere as I was thinking about how to solve the problems of the universe, and when I snapped out of it, I found that I was looking right at a red-bearded biker. How long had I been looking at him? I had to say something quick. "Nice tattoos."

"Thanks, bro."

"So, uh, who did them?"

"Most of 'em I did myself. Hey, if you know anyone who wants any, send 'em down to me in Venice."

Here was a likely proposition. I can just imagine getting a Harley Davidson tattoo from this guy and him talking about all the bisexual Haitians he just got done tattooing with the same needle he's using on me and wondering about what those strange spots on them were.

"Who should I send them to? I don't know your name."

"Ugly."

"Huh?"

"Ugly. That's my name. It's tattooed right here on my arm," he said, pointing to the tat.

I talked myself away from him and went outside for some air. The

Domino's Pizza guy was delivering next door. I bonded with him mentally.

When the door opened, they asked him to come in while they got their money together. I didn't want to leave him, so I turned myself invisible and followed him in. I sat next to the Domino's guy on the couch. A red-eyed guy was foraging around the apartment for money. On a futon, two girls slept.

The futon cover was zebra striped, so I spent quite some time staring at it, until I heard the door close. The pizza guy was gone. Suddenly, I realized I was no longer invisible. This was bad. My mind shifted between "I hope they don't call the cops" and "I wonder if they'll give me a slice." In one of the panicking phases, I stood up, introduced myself, and ran out the door. I'm still not sure if they ever saw me.

I got back and the bikers had gone, along with everyone else except for about twenty people. Norris, a forty year old hippie, yakked his tofu in the middle of the room. This got the remainder of the people out of there.

Norris went outside to get some air. Someone who was walking by hacked a loogie and spit. Norris, in his suggestible state, urped and spat something vile that made Linda Blair look weak. It wasn't really a vomit, it was a spit, but it was about a pint of soupy yellowish green barfage. That's when I knew that I better not stick around to let things get any worse.

I passed Methuselah on the way over to Ron. He was lying face down on the floor saying "Go home" over and over.

When we got to Ron and Dennis' house, The Magical Mystery Trip Through Little Red's Head came on TV and after we watched it, and they crashed, I stayed up for a while staring at Ron's Jim Morrison poster, waiting for the lips to part and the spirit of Jim to tell me secrets from beyond the grave.

MARIO, THE NINE-FINGERED USED CAR LOT CLOWN

"I want the red one!"

"Me, too!"

"No, give it to me!"

The children jumped all over Mario. They pulled, tugged, and tried to climb up his clothing to get to the balloons he had. Sweat made his clownface makeup and his red rubber nose itch.

"Awright, awright," he boomed. "There's only one red one left and only one of ya's gonna get it so cool it unless you want me to let it go into the wild blue yonder."

He gave each of them a balloon and the kids ran off to their parents across the lot by the minivans and station wagons, all except one child who looked about eight years old.

"Hey, mister," he squinted. "What happened to your missing finger?"

"It got bit off by a clown. Now beat it, runt."

The child bolted away, screaming "Mommmmyyyyyyyy!"

Two families, Mario thought, what could be worse than two families coming at once? Mario stepped behind a camper and reached for his cigarettes. They were gone. This was too much. Mario stormed over to the two couples and Jack, the lot owner.

"This one's got a lot a mileage, but it's got--" Jack proudly lied as Mario interrupted him.

"Little monsters!"

"Mario, what are you talking about?" Jack panicked. "This minivan is flawless!"

"Not the van, you shmuck, their kids!"

The couples stuttered, speechless in their astonishment.

"Your sticky-fingered little brats," Mario accused, pointing a finger in their faces, "stole my cigarettes!"

Jack knew Mario was serious. Even through the clown face, the fighting face from his boxing days was churning. He got between Mario and the couples and pushed the clown back behind the camper. "Excuse me, folks, I'll be right with you."

Once they were out of sight, Jack's face became the color of Mario's fake nose. "What the hell do you think you're doing? I can make a double sale here! I can play these jackasses against each other and they'll buy the two most expensive cars on my lot trying to outdo each other! Tell me! What the hell do you think you are doing?"

Mario said nothing, just reached into Jack's shirt pocket with his four-fingered right hand that once made many men unconscious, flipped up the lid to his cigarettes, took one out, and stuck it in his mouth. Mario still had his lighter. He lit up, took a drag, and blew a mouthful of warning smoke into Jack's face.

Jack's veins went back into his neck as he got the message. He took out his handkerchief. "Why don't you take an early lunch?" he begged, wiping his forehead.

Mario gave him a nod and left the lot, heading across the street to his cousin Frank's pizza place where he could always eat free and the tomato sauce was made from Grandma's secret recipe.

Mario had a hard time finding work. To him, the most shameful man was the unemployed man. Better to have a humiliating job than none at all.

Mario pushed open the door to Frank's place. He was the only customer, but that would only last for thirty minutes or so. Then the lunch rush would hit.

"A man deserves a good job!" Mario boomed as he pushed open the restaurant door. A teenage employee who was wiping tables jumped, startled at his usual entrance.

"Good morning, Mario!" Frank yelled from the kitchen. "You're here early today. You didn't get canned, did you?"

Mario went to a table that was still wet and sat down. The teenager looked over in contempt between wipes.

"This guy is always such a sloppy pig," she muttered.

Mario took off his red nose and stuck it on the salt shaker. He blotted his face carefully with a napkin, so as not to remove his makeup.

"Where's a man's dignity in a lousy job?" Mario moaned.

"Where's a man's dignity in a lousy job?" the table-wiper mouthed along silently in unison.

"I know, I know, dear cousin. You know you're welcome to a job here anytime," Frank calmly reassured. The girl wiping tables started cleaning more thoroughly. Not my job, you nine-fingered geezer, she thought.

"Frankie boy, as my last living relative in the state, and as my little cousin, I'm not going to leech off you. Hey, how's the sausage today?"

"Fresh, Mario, as usual, how about testing a few slices for me?"

"Sure thing, Frankie, anything for family."

Frank went into the kitchen as Mario watched the door and spun the basil shaker. The door opened and several families walked in, small children first and then the rest. They sat at the long table which went down the center of the floor. One by one, he watched the chairs fill up with children, the pride of their parents sitting beside them. The people looked familiar, but Mario was positive he knew the older man who was with them.

"Hey, hey, Luzinski!" Mario yelled. "Over here, ya goon! It's me, Mario Cortelli, from high school!"

Sam Luzinski looked over at Mario, squinted, and smiled. He came over, stood by his table, and extended his hand. Mario stuck out his right hand to meet it, and when they shook, Sam Luzinski got the look on his face that a man only gets when he shakes a man's hand and some of the fingers are missing. Mario knew the look only too well.

"I lost a finger a long time ago. I thought you knew. Word got around pretty quick."

"Sorry," Sam said uncomfortably. He thought of something to change the subject. "Say, uh, how come I stopped seeing your name in the papers?

What happened to your boxing career?"

Mario blew out the last of his cigarette smoke and crushed the butt in the ashtray. He held up his right hand.

"It takes five fingers to make a fist, Luzinski. I went off into boxing, was doing pretty well, and then some hood tells me he can make me rich if I take a fall for him. Course I told the jerk to get lost. I don't take no falls, I got my pride, I told him. But you ain't got no career, he said, and called in a couple of his boys and they cut off the finger."

Sam looked at the ground. "What a shame," he said, "You were tough as nails, Mario, tough as nails."

"What happened to you, Mr. Quarterback, huh? I didn't see your name on the sports pages either."

"Well, Mario," he smiled, "As you know, in our day being a pro football player wasn't so much of a privilege. I got a scholarship to State and even got drafted by the Colts in the late rounds, but I had also gotten a degree in business and went off to New York City to make my fortune. I haven't been back here in about thirty years."

Mario made a could-I-have-a-cigarette pantomime and Sam gave him one. Mario lit up.

"Thanks," he said, puffing away. "What the hell are ya doing back here anyway?"

Sam looked at him with a bit of surprise. "Why, our forty-year high school reunion, of course. You're going, aren't you?"

Forty years? Mario thought. Yeah, he was fifty-seven years old, sure enough. All that time and nothing...

"Nah," he shrugged. "Those things always bore me."

"C'mon, what's a reunion going to be without Luzinski and Corletti, star quarterback-center duo of the State Champion Mustangs?"

Cortelli, you sentimental jackass, the name's Cortelli, Mario thought.

"I guess I'll show up for a while. Hey, are all these your family?"

"Yes," he beamed. "My two kids and my five grandchildren. Hey, they live here in town, actually, maybe you've met them."

Mario looked over at the people. Suddenly he realized who they were. The people from the car lot.

"We've met before," Mario slurred.

"Okay, great. Well, I'm going to get back to them now. See you at the reunion, huh? And maybe you should be getting more sun," he said with a wink and a grin.

Mario nodded goodbye, confused slightly, and then remembered his makeup. He laughed in spite of his embarrassment at being caught in such a costume.

Frank's sole employee reluctantly brought him two large slices of sausage pizza. Mario got up and went to wash his hands, ignoring stares and giggles.

The bathroom reeked of his brand of cigarettes. Mario could see two pairs of little feet and legs under the stall door. He washed his hands listening to two voices argue about how to smoke like a man.

He left, and when he passed Sam's table he yelled, "Hey, Luzinski, one of your little angels got hisself stuck in the john."

"Thanks, Mario," he said, smiling, and went to the bathroom.

Mario sat down, watching the bathroom doors. He took a bite of the pizza, almost as good as Grandma's, as usual. You can't touch Grandma though, never have, never will, he thought, not even with her personal recipes. A pizza to be proud to call your own, nonetheless.

The men's room door nearly came off its hinges when Sam came out, dragging two little boys, eight and nine years old, by their arms.

"Smoking! These little monsters were smoking in there! Where did they get cigarettes from, anyway?"

The two boys were crying, the parents were speechless and embarrassed, and the rest of the children were laughing as the whole restaurant was staring. Anxious whispering went on among the parents.

"Why don't we go home? We haven't ordered yet," one mother said, looking embarrassed, and the rest agreed. They filed out the door, the two boys still crying, the parents still flustered, and the rest of the children still laughing. Sam caught Mario's eye right before he went out.

"See you at the reunion?"

Mario nodded, but wasn't sure. He dropped his fork on the floor and went up to the front for another one.

Three teenage boys were playing pinball and flirting with the girl as she refilled the straw dispenser.

"Hey, if it ain't Stubby the Clown," an obnoxious voice taunted, and they all laughed. Mario ignored them.

"Hey, Stubby! Hey, Stubby! Yoo-hoo, ya deaf or sumpin?"

Mario turned to face them. The one who was talking was Taylor, Jack's son who was in the Marines. He was nineteen and just back from boot camp.

"You got a big mouth, kid."

"You know what they say about what really happened to your tenth finger?" his boss's son said with a mean grin. He glanced conspiratorially at his companions.

"I don't give a damn what they say," Mario lied. He knew kids told each other cruel things about him and his finger, dirty, mean things, but he didn't know exactly what. He now realized the whole restaurant was watching.

"Ooooh, tough talk for a clown," Taylor said with a laugh. "Whaddya going to do, old man, honk your horn at me?" The three kids laughed.

"In my day, we were taught to respect our elders."

"Too bad we're not in your day," Taylor retorted.

"Don't bet on it, kid," Mario said, his left hand forming a fist. He punched Taylor in the nose and heard a smack and a snap. The smack was his fist, and the snap was the smartass's nose breaking. Taylor spun and landed face down on the floor. He didn't move and a puddle of blood was forming.

The two kids bolted for the door. Some of the customers were laughing, and a few applauding.

"Always a fucking mess," the employee wailed.

"Mario, Mario, dear Cousin Mario, what in the name of Heaven have you done?" Frank panicked. "You'll get fired from the car lot for this! Don't you know how hard it is to get work these days?"

Mario turned without a word to anyone and walked out the door, leaving his red rubber nose on the salt shaker.

LIVING ON METHEDRINE TIME

Living on methedrine time
Minutes pass by too fast to breathe
Hours pass like strangers
Days are identical septuplets

The world is recreated each moment
A little more cruel each time
A little more harsh each time
A little more diabolical each time

More places each time to hide you
More ways to beat you down
More millstones for your neck

Seems like you just got that new tattoo yesterday
It's faded now
Or maybe it's just you
I haven't seen you around lately
But I always haven't seen you around lately
You been gone
or just harder to see?
What've you been up to?
Running through your life
missing all your big breaks?

Could've been somebody if
there'd only been more time
Could've been somebody if
the band had stayed together
Could've been somebody if
the guitar hadn't been sold
But all that was a long time ago

and if you could talk about it
for minimum wage
you would've made rent this month
But as it is
the landlord's ripping off pages
of the thirty day countdown to couch trip tour calendar
and no one seems to be around anymore—

Where's all those people
you helped out?
Where's all those people
you lent money to?
Where's all those people
who crashed at your house?
Where is anyone you know for that matter?
Where did everyone go that used to hang out all the time?
And why didn't they ask you to come along?

She moved back to Indiana
He shot himself in the head
She ran her bike into a bus
He jumped out of a window
She who wore her club stamps like track marks
traded in her club stamps for track marks
and like all speed freaks
she didn't die
she just got thinner and thinner
until she rolled up on herself like a cartoon window shade

All these strangers
at your hangout
who are they?
why don't they want to know
who you are?

You don't talk like them
you don't act like them
you don't look like them
and you couldn't if you tried
You're marked by your generation
tribal markings of the modern primitive dinosaurs
shut out
shoved out
and fossilized
part of another revolution
born bred and died
and nothing ever changed
A quick fuck in the ass
without a kiss or a reach around
is all it was

You'd feel more in place
in the rehab clinics or mental hospitals
or in your parent's basement
talking to the last of your brain cells about
"Back when things were cool"

Now you're left behind
to watch the next bunch of freshies
move into town
plan their own cultural revolution
go do their dances
trying to catch the ultimate experience
with the enthusiastic desperation
of a junkie chasing after the ultimate high
It all sounds so familiar
you want to tell them
shake them
and warn them
but they wouldn't believe you

Time has pinned your arms back
Beauty has one hand around your neck
Your eyes bulge looking at her
Bloodshot lovers
You don't dare blink
But she's got an eyeball crowbar
in her other hand
and when she smiles
she's got retinas in her teeth
and optic nerves on her breath
Now you know
what beauty eats
Now you know
the sound of time laughing
Now you know
how it feels to be the fatted calf
Now you know
as the last grain of sanity falls to the bottom of the hourglass
that the cutting edge
will slice you to shreds

BLOOD VIRGIN

I asked him what I was going to hunt with
and when he put the thirty aught six in my hands
it was his way of saying
"You are a man now."

In the light morning rain
she walked home
afraid of the rain
like a child is afraid of the dark
she could not smell me but I saw her many times
through the drops on my glasses
and when I saw her in the scope
I knew she was mine.

I shot her once and she kicked
pain-ridden and desperate
the second shot
she heard but never felt
kicked some more
it was the first time for both of us
the third shot
and she lay still
waiting for me.

I stood over her
knife drawn
and the guilty look in her eye
said "You are a man now."

I had just started on her
when I heard footsteps.
It was my father.

He watched over my shoulder
as I breathed the steam from her open body
telling me where to cut and when
but I would've known anyway.
The little talk came a little too late.
It was the closest we had ever been
but all the same I wanted to be alone.

They named that clearing in Kentucky after me.
They should've named it after her
too.

THE JESUS VIRUS

If you were unfortunate enough
to be lonely or depressed in Boston in the mid-eighties,
especially if you went to malls,
chances are
I came up to you and
offered to be your best friend.

My friends and I
were infecting the town the best we could
with the Jesus virus.
Our ultimate plan was for the world,
but right now
it was going to be the Natick Mall or Quincy Market.

We'd meet up beforehand,
get our pep talks that resembled lines of speed,
and assigned our quotas,
take off in pairs,
always a veteran with a rookie.

Such easy targets...
like animals with bull's-eye fur patterns
from one shoe store away,
we could tell who wanted to be talked to,
who needed an answer,
and believe me
we had all the answers you'd ever need.

Give us a minute, we'd take an hour.
Give us an hour, we'd take a day.
Give us a day, we'd take a weekend.
Give us a weekend, we'd take your whole damn life away,

and you would be out recruiting with us next week,
dangling carrots of bliss in front of faces.
The answers and the companionship were there,
but there was no time to really question them
because I was always a little bit behind quota
and late for a meeting,
and since I was in high school
and working twenty hours a week
while going to at least fifteen hours a week of church meetings,
I was just a little too tired to give a damn
about whether or not I was right.
I just wanted to sleep
and was looking forward to tomorrow
when the forty-eight hour fast was going to end.
Just about that time something would pop up
like an all-night Friday prayer meeting.

I still catch myself
sizing up people in a crowd.
Finding targets,
people that would listen to me for five minutes
and come on a weekend retreat with me.
I leave them alone now,
try not to think about them,
but it pisses me off knowing how easily
they could walk right into it,
catch the Jesus virus,
or the Krishna plague,
or Moon disease,
like they were licking a bus station toilet seat
because it's that easy
and I only wish it were that obvious.

THE BITTERNESS I TASTE IS NOT FROM MY BARLEY

I took a drink but all I got was ashes
the butts were your brand

didn't think you'd be seen in a place like this
didn't think you'd risk people like me
    drinking after you

if we are both here all night
we will not be in the same room
    but watching each other
    like looking in the neighbor's window

    Is that me over there
        talking to you
    Is that me over there
        fighting with you
    Is that me over there
        having sex with you
    Is that me over there
        or is it you

We will interact,
    simultaneously becoming voyeurs
    standing outside our bodies
        next to each other
        backs turned
    As our corpses become congenial
        we become nauseous

    I need a drink
        to keep talking to you
    I need a drink

to keep fighting with you
I need a drink
to fornicate with you
I need a drink
how about you

I look around this place.
I see no one to talk to.
No one else will understand the horror
of being in love with you
No one else will understand the horror
of being in love with me
so we're stuck with each other
incestuous Siamese twin Volkswagen Beetles
in a lover's spat
using each other for spare parts.

The bitterness I taste is not from my barley
so could you buy me a beer
to wash it all down?

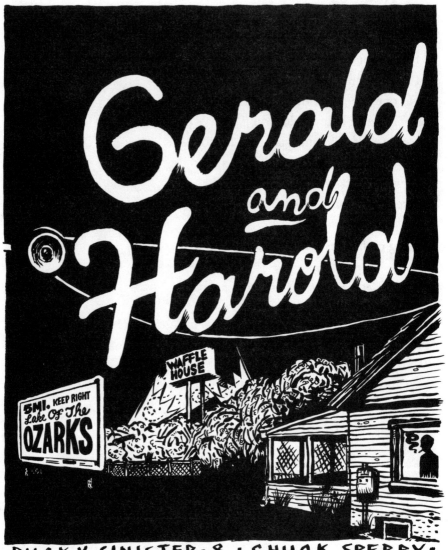

Gerald and Harold were brothers. They were twins, sort of.

When Gerald was born they tried to clone an exact duplicate,

but something went wrong, terribly wrong,

horribly wrong, some might say,

and Harold never grew to be more than six inches long

and he had suction cups all over his body.

Gerald hated Harold because Harold got all the attention. When their parents were gone, he'd lick Harold all over and stick him up on the living room window.

On their sixteenth birthday, Gerald got his revenge. He got a brand new Trans Am. Harold, being too small to drive, got a pair of socks. Harold looked up at his brother from the sofa.

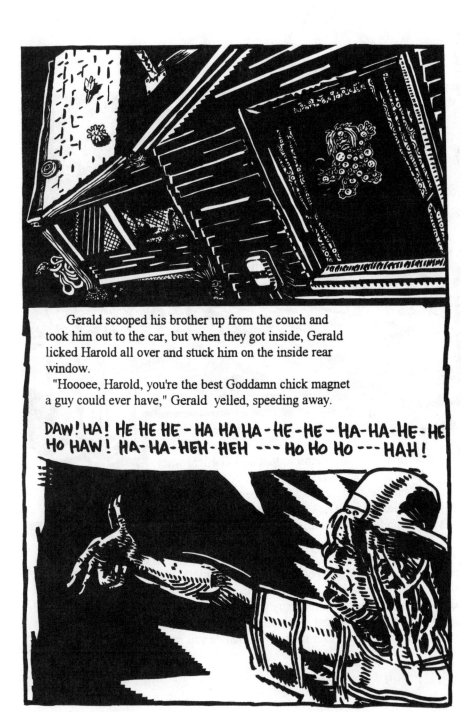

Gerald scooped his brother up from the couch and took him out to the car, but when they got inside, Gerald licked Harold all over and stuck him on the inside rear window.

"Hoooee, Harold, you're the best Goddamn chick magnet a guy could ever have," Gerald yelled, speeding away.

When they got to Tastee Freeze, two girls came up to the car.

"Hey, that ain't Bart Simpson, that ain't Garfield what the heck is that?" they puzzled.

"That's my brother Harold," Gerald exclaimed, "he's only six inches long and he's got suction cups all over his body, and he's for real, he's alive."

The two girls looked at each other in awe. Then they looked back at Gerald.

"Gerald, we got a fifth bottle full of Jack Daniel's whiskey and we're looking to share it with a guy just like you. We want to share it with a guy who's got a brand new Trans Am and a brother who's only six inches long and has suction cups all over his body. What do you say, Gerald ..."

YOU GONNA TAKE US FOR A RIDE?

SK-REEEE

Nothing more needed to be said. The girls got in and they all sped away.

Now everyone was laughing and singing and drinking and having a good time. Everyone but little Harold, that is. He was still stuck up on the window and was thinking to himself, you know, I might only be six inches long, and I might have suction cups all over my body, but tonight I'm sixteen years old and I deserve to have a good time just like anyone else. I can't help the way I was born now can I? Meanwhile, the Jack Daniel's bottle had emptied, and with it, Gerald's reaction time and judgement were down to nothing.

When they approached the tracks, the girls looked at Gerald and said,

THE PALE RIDER

Gerald looked in the rear view mirror at his brother stuck on the window, thought about it, and said,

THAT TRAIN'S COMING GERALD, BUT WE WANT YOU TO BEAT THAT TRAIN, BECAUSE ONLY A REAL MAN CAN BEAT A TRAIN. AND WE PUT OUT FOR REAL MEN. WHAT DO YOU SAY, GERALD?

I'M GOING TO BEAT THAT TRAIN, I'M GOING TO BEAT THAT TRAIN, BECAUSE TO-NIGHT I'M SIXTEEN YEARS OLD, WITH A BELLY FULL OF JACK DANIELS WISKEY AND A BRAND NEW TRANS AM, AND I'M A MAN, I'M A MAN I'M A MAN

But he wasn't man enough, because that train beat Gerald, and when the paramedics came, they couldn't tell the girls from Gerald, the girls from each other, the car from Gerald, the girls from the car, everyone was really fucked up. Everyone except little Harold, that is, and he wasn't doing too well.

They could hear Harold whispering something. They carefully unsuckered him, and held him up to their ears.

HAPPY BIRTHDAY. HAPPY CRAZY FUCKING GODDAMN BIRTHDAY.

MERCUROCHROME

I crawled out of the lake this morning and headed home to wash up. I was covered with mud and cut all over. My jaw hurt.

It was dawn and my Keds squished. I took the main road home and no one was out as usual. The first time I walked that way it seemed to take forever but I've traveled that route every morning for so long I'm used to it now.

I got to the house and there was Daddy, swinging from the tree like he always does. His neck was bent and he'd wet his pants. His eyes were real messed up, I couldn't even look at them long enough to describe them.

I went inside and Grandpa was sitting in the living room watching TV as usual. Grandpa was a rodeo clown. Still is, mostly. It's all he ever talks about. He was smoking and drinking beer and the cans surrounded his chair. All he wore was his boxers and his clownface. In the blue glow from the set, I could see the scars through his makeup. They were all over the rest of his body. My favorite one is the huge round one on his stomach from the bull horn. He tells the gore story over and over.

While I was watching TV with Grandpa, my little brother came dragging himself through the living room as usual. He lay down on his stomach and propped himself up on his front arms and watched the show. Some old movie was on. I had to leave because I can't stand to look at him. It's not that I don't like my brother, it's more that dumb smile and his broken hip bone that make me so sick.

I got into the bathroom. It's the only clean room in the house, and that's because of me. I started the bath water running. I took off all my clothes and put some things by the tub: some of Grandpa's smokes, a lighter, and a bottle of mercurochrome.

The water turned brown as soon as I got in. When I washed away the mud, I saw all my cuts underneath. I put some mercurochrome on them. Somewhere else in the house, I heard a woman's voice. It made me think of grownups and how stupid they are.

I lit a cigarette and took a deep inhale. It made me feel heavy. The sunlight coming in through the window was almost to the sink. I watched it crawl across the green tiles until it hit the marbleized sink.

I pretended the sink handles were diamonds, the way the light shattered off them. The light and the smokes are my only treasures. Once a day, every day, I go through the same routine. It's these few minutes that let me face the rest. I pretend that there are steel poles around the bathtub, a cage keeping me safe from all the rest of this hell.

I knew Daddy would be slipping out of the noose again soon because I could hear the dogs barking. He would pull me out of the tub, make me get dressed, and take me for a ride in the Mopar. Then he would pull out his dick and make me suck it and I would have to stare at that sacred heart tattoo on his thigh. When he was done with me, he'd throw me in the lake, and by the time I got home, he would be swinging from the tree in the front yard again.

The room got hotter as Grandpa fell asleep and set the house on fire with a burning cigarette again and I heard Daddy's footsteps on the stairway. Deep in my heart, I knew it was time for me to leave, but deeper still, I knew there was no place to go.

ARKANSAS SUMMER

For one final summer, the woods filled themselves with imaginary Nazi stormtroopers for me and my three best friends to search out and destroy with plastic machine guns. We were all eleven years old and thought that life would never change.

Normally in rural Arkansas, magazines or television would be the only places you'd see an exotic car like the candy-apple red Porsche we saw on one of the first days of summer vacation. When we saw it, we were at our secret hideout in the woods, a place not even our parents knew about.

The hideout was no more than a lean-to, built on a ridge that overlooked the highway, which was how we were able to scout for invading troops, or Porsches running out of gas, whichever the case may have been. Although they were both almost as likely never to happen, the latter did. Chuck pointed it out with a squeak.

"Porsche!" he said, and swallowed hard and said it again. "Hey, guys! It's a Porsche!"

We knew by the sound of his voice that it was not a joke, and we all rushed to where he was to get a good look.

"Christ on a cross," Eddie breathed in a low tone of reverence. "It really is a Porsche."

Eddie was the leader of the group, being the strongest, the fastest, and the only one who not only knew all twenty-seven cuss words but knew what they meant. He said them quite often and made them sound quite natural. The rest of us didn't cuss much because when we did we never picked the right words so besides sounding awkward we didn't make any sense.

"A real, live, honest-to-goodness Porsche," followed William.

In addition to being whiny, William was small for his age so no one at school liked him, not even us sometimes, but we all grew up together and never thought about doing anything without the other three. Many times Chuck, Eddie, and I came to his rescue on the playground. Even some of the younger kids were bigger and picked on him.

Chuck and I were still staring in awe when Eddie said, "Let's get a closer look."

The driver had gotten out and walked down the road to get gas, and by now he was around the bend and out of sight. Eddie scampered down the gravel trail that led to the highway. Chuck and I immediately followed with William lagging way behind.

"Slow down, guys, I might slip and fall," he moaned.

"Shut up, William," came back a chorus of replies.

Within seconds we were standing next to the car of our dreams, afraid to touch it because it might vanish like a mirage if we did. We were quiet, like questing pilgrims in front of a holy artifact, our plastic weapons hanging loosely on our backs from homemade kite string straps. I looked at the immaculate paint job, caressed the smooth curves. I had to know what the car driven by a god on Earth felt like: would it feel like ice but warm, or would it be like touching a sunset? My hand reached out but jerked back when William shrieked.

"Wait!" he warned as he lowered his gun and pointed at the car. "Aren't these cars made in Germany?"

"For cryin' out loud, William," I said. "We aren't playin' right now. World War II ended over thirty years ago. Besides half of Germany is the good guys now."

I extended my hand again until my palm was flat on the surface. It felt smooth, unlike my father's Buick, and my hand led me around the car as the others joined in the touching with me.

"Let's break in!" Eddie blurted.

"No!" William screamed in shock. "We'll get in a lot of trouble."

"Shut up, William," Eddie started. "Don't be such a..."

"No, Eddie, this time, he's right," I stated, with Chuck nodding in agreement.

"Who's gonna know?" Eddie asked. "You can hear cars coming a long way off, and even if that guy went to the closest gas station he won't be back for at least forty-five minutes."

We didn't budge.

"Come on, guys, think about it." He was trying his best to convince us. "Anyone who drives a machine like this might have a lot of money inside, like a hundred bucks."

Now we were all in favor of it but we realized that none of us knew how to break into a car, so after some debate, Eddie picked up a rock and smashed the window with a sound louder than we'd thought possible for glass to make but not near as loud as the alarm that started going off.

William ran halfway back up the trail when he realized we weren't following and came back down. He started jumping up and down and screaming at us to leave. Chuck and I were frozen in place and Eddie was trying to get the door unlocked. The door came open, and Eddie shot into the front seat, rifling through any compartment he could find, being cautious of all the broken glass.

"Help me look, goddamit!" he yelled. "We ain't got all day!"

I got the seat up and started to look in the back seat as Chuck helped search the front and William continued his screaming.

"Al Jarreau? Barry Manilow?" said Chuck as he tossed tape after tape out of the car. "Hasn't this guy ever heard of good music, like Kiss?"

That's when I stuck my hand into a suede pouch in back of the passenger seat and felt a cold metal tube. I reluctantly wrapped my fingers around it and started to pull it into sight. Chuck and Eddie were out of the car already and even Eddie was ready to leave.

"Let's go, there's nuthin' here but pocket change, which I got, and stupid disco..." He stopped as I held up a nickel-plated forty-four magnum pistol and let my mouth hang open.

"Holy shit," he whispered. "A gun!"

The road started to rumble with the sound of an approaching eighteen-wheeler so we ran back to our hideout. I was still holding the pistol by the barrel.

When we got to the hideout, I put the gun down in the center of us and we all just looked at it, breathing heavily from the run. The same thoughts went through our heads. Before now, our most prized possession was the Playboy magazine Chuck had stolen from his cousin, and now we had a gun of our own. This meant we weren't kids anymore. Having a gun meant manhood. We all had shot a gun many times and even went hunting with our fathers once in a while, but none of us owned anything bigger than a pellet gun, not even any of the guys we knew at school. But this was tremendously more than a pellet gun or even a .22: this was the gun owned by Dirty Harry.

The way the weapon caught sunlight made it look like it was shining in holy radiance. It was truly a gift from the heavens, sent to liberate us from childhood. But, as usual, Eddie broke our mystical revelation with a question we were all thinking.

"All right, who gets to keep it?"

We argued for a while about taking turns and how long turns should be. It was finally decided that each of us would get it for a day, but everyone wanted it first, so we settled things the way we always did: potato-knocking.

As always, Eddie was the knocker. Chuck went out before I even lost a potato fist and I was sweating not from the heat, but from the anticipation that I would get the gun first, but I was the next one out. Eddie depressingly knocked himself out, leaving William the joyous victor. He immediately jumped up, screamed, and did a football-player-in-the-end-zone victory dance as the rest of us tried to pretend that we didn't notice or care, but it was all we cared about.

Soon enough, we were playing World War II again down by the creek. I was thinking how assassinating Hitler day after day for years was getting old when William made a ludicrous suggestion.

"Let's play something else now," he said, waving his nickel-plated prize in the air, "like Cops and Robbers."

"Cops and Robbers is for babies," I told him. "We haven't played that since we were little."

Eddie and Chuck agreed, but William insisted in a sing-song voice, "You gotta do what I say now, 'cause I've got the gu-un."

"Shut up, you little prick," Eddie blurted out. "That doesn't count for jackshit and you fucking know it."

Chuck and I started to laugh and William's face turned red with embarrassment. Eddie joined in the laughter until William's lip started to quiver and a tear rolled out of his left eye.

"Christ," Eddie exclaimed. "What a fucking baby."

That comment only forced more tears to flow. With shaking hands, William lifted the gun and pointed it at Eddie.

"Take that back, Eddie," he whimpered, "or I'll blow your brains out."

This only made us laugh harder. Chuck and I were on the ground, rolling around and beating our fists in the leaves and dirt.

"Yeah, right," Eddie said. "You're going to shoot me. Give me the fucking gun, you wuss." Eddie started advancing towards William, as if to take the gun from him.

"Not any closer," warned William, the gun shaking more than ever. "Don't come any closer or I'll shoot."

Eddie laughed and moved closer. Chuck now had his hands on his stomach and was crying from laughter as we both watched and filled the near-isolated woods with noise.

But we were not as loud as the exploding gunshot. I was looking at Eddie, and the back part of his head shattered from a bullet entering his forehead. The force lifted him up and sent him crashing to the ground in what seemed like slow motion. In my peripheral vision, I saw the kick of the shot send the gun backwards so that the hammer struck William hard in the forehead. Chuck and I immediately quit laughing. The woods were suddenly quiet again as if nature was ignoring us. William was the only one to get up. He had blood coming down his face but didn't seem to care.

"Eddie," he called, and rushed over to where Eddie lay. He sat on Eddie's abdomen, straddling the lifeless body, his knees touching the dry dirt of the ground. He tugged on Eddie's blood-soaked shirt with clenched fists. The smell was unbelievable: a pinching odor of old pennies. Nausea was wringing my guts, and to this day I have never smelled anything worse.

"Eddie, get up. Eddie, get up. Eddie, get up," he repeated, shaking the body around, trying to shake life into stale glass eyes.

"Eddie, say something," William pleaded, but Eddie's gaping mouth refused to move.

Chuck and I were in shock, but we managed to walk over.

"William," I said, "let's go. There's nothing we can do for him now." We led William to the lean-to and sat him down. Chuck and I went off to talk.

"What now, Chuck?" I asked.

"First of all, we've got to do something about the body. We can either try to cover this whole thing up, or we can tell the truth. The way I see it, even though it was an accident, that's hard to prove. William will do time either way," Chuck reasoned.

The idea of going to jail, even if it was juvie hall, was horrifying, but I was not so sure about the point that it was an accident. Of course, we both knew William would not want to kill anyone. He was just scared and upset. But did that make it an accident? I didn't think so, but I did perceive this as a wild exception. William was not a dangerous person that should be locked up.

"And then there's our involvement," Chuck continued calmly. "We're accessories or something. We'd definitely at least get busted for breaking into the Porsche."

Now I knew for sure that he was right. We could all be put in the slammer for this.

"I say we hide the body then," I said. Chuck agreed and we returned to the hideout to get the collapsible field shovel, leaving William crumpled over and crying as we went back to Eddie's body. We talked about a burial place and decided the creek would be the best place, since it was closest. On the way to the creek with the body, Chuck softly commented, "On television people die with their eyes closed."

We took off our shoes and socks and rolled our pantlegs up, and took turns digging. When we had gotten three or four feet deep, we decided to put the body in.

"Wait," Chuck said. He ran off and came back with the gun and threw it into the watery hole.

We lowered Eddie into the grave and covered him up. With the water passing over, you couldn't tell anything had been bothered. Chuck and I started throwing up, almost because it seemed like a good idea. It was the strangest vomit I had ever seen. Those half-digested chunks were our childhoods floating away forever.

We got our shoes and socks back on and went to the hideout. William was still there, and he had stopped crying. He was staring into the trees with that same glassy-eyed look Eddie had.

"Let's go home, William," I said, my arm around him. "It's going to be all right. We've taken care of everything."

Chuck and I walked him home. Right before we got to his house William started to cry. His mom heard and came outside and asked us what happened and how did he get blood on his face which we thought was the same question. Chuck told her that he fell out of a tree. She took him inside and we walked home.

Chuck and I lived on the same street. We got to his house first and I walked on.

"See ya tomorrow," he said.

"Yeah, I guess," I replied without looking at him.

I walked into my house through the back door. My mom was the only one home.

"For Pete's sake," she said, wrinkling her nose. "Go take a bath and get out of those clothes. What have you been into? You smell like death warmed over."

I didn't say a word. I just walked back to the bathroom, pausing briefly in the hallway to look at my baby pictures displayed on the wall. I looked so different then, so innocent or something.

I peeled off my creekwater-soaked clothes, letting the plastic machine gun on my back clatter to the floor. I stood in the shower and just let the water strike me. For once I actually used the soap because I wanted to feel clean.

That night at dinner, my parents got a phone call from Eddie's dad asking if he was over there or if we had seen him. I lied and said that he had never showed up today with the other guys.

It rained that night and all the next day as if the earth wanted to clean itself.

The next evening on the local news, there was a story about Eddie and how his parents thought that he may have been kidnapped. They organized search parties and put up flyers with his picture and their phone number on them. From what they said on television, they were searching the completely wrong area of the woods.

Chuck called me the next morning and asked if I wanted to go to the hideout. I said I didn't feel like it and he said that was good because he didn't want to go either.

My parents were really worried about me. One morning Mom didn't notice that Eddie's picture was on the milk carton at the breakfast table. When I saw it, I threw it across the kitchen and ran out of the house. No one said a word to me or even asked where I was going.

I went down to Chuck's house for the first time in two weeks. There was a hole in one of the garbage bags in front of the house and I saw the plastic barrel of a gun sticking out. Suddenly I didn't feel so stupid about throwing mine away.

Chuck's mom let me in, and I saw him watching a game show. He saw me and turned it off.

"Let's go back to my room," he said. We went back and shut the door.

"Long time no see," he said.

"Yeah."

"You spoken to William yet?" he asked.

"No."

"I didn't for a while, because I didn't know what to say. I went over a few days ago anyway. His mom and dad sent him to live with his uncle in Florida for a while. His mom told me that ever since he fell out of the tree, he won't talk to anyone anymore. She said he'll be back, but she has no idea when. Maybe a couple of years, even."

We both stared at the floor.

"You heard about the new warehouse?" he asked.

"No."

"Some company is going to build a huge warehouse and distribution center here because the land is so cheap. And guess where? Right over our hideout all the way to where Eddie is buried. Pretty soon that whole place will be concrete. The new president is moving in pretty close to us in that new two-story house on Crabtree Lane."

We were quiet again.

"Mom said reporters would come by to talk to us about how we feel about Eddie being missing but that we don't have to talk to them if we don't feel like it."

"Look," I said, "I'm not feeling well, I'm going home."

"All right," he said. "Come on by later if you want to. *The Dirty Dozen* is on TV tonight."

"Okay," I said. "See ya later."

"Yeah."

I walked past my house down to Crabtree Lane. There was a big U-Haul moving van parked out front and a bright red Porsche in the driveway. I went to get a closer look and was noticing that one of the windows had been broken out, when a kid who looked eight or nine years old came around the corner of the moving van.

"Get away from my car," he demanded, and shot me four or five times with a fancy cap gun made to look like a forty-four magnum pistol. I grabbed the gun from him, knocked him down, threw the gun on the roof, and ran all the way home.

ASPHALT RIVERS

The rain turns the street below
into a river
that reflects the neon leaves
of the overhanging concrete tree branches.

Like the pigeons that have been forced to their holes
I watch the rain from my window
feeling like an eroded gargoyle.

My youth washes into my past
like a cigarette butt into the sewer,
and the rain keeps falling,
as if it will never stop.

TOASTER THERAPY

I bought a loaf of bread,
took it home,
turned off all the lights,
and started toasting the slices two by two,
dedicating each slice
to someone or some group of people
who tried to make my life a hell.

I pushed the button down
and watched the coils glow and char the helpless slices.
I ate each piece,
as if I were consuming their attempt to slow me down.
I started to laugh because I had won the game
I never wanted to play in the first place.
I knew that everything was not perfect,
but my stomach was filling up
and the bread crumbs burning smelled like victory.

With the last two slices,
I picked someone really deserving
and set the toaster all the way to the hottest setting.
I hate the way burnt toast tastes,
but it crunched in my mouth like tiny skeletons
and I liked the way the smoke curled into nowhere
like souls tearing themselves apart.

And I thought about how
one of these days,
I'm going to buy a roomful of toasters
and toast the whole loaf at once.

FOR A FRIEND IN THE SAND

I saw him break an acoustic guitar over his head
like he was christening a ship.
I saw him bid goodbye to his soccer ball
and kick it into the ocean.

He got into fights
almost every day in high school.
People told me he was a bad influence
and not to hang out with him.

People talked a lot
but people weren't my friend.
He was.
He was the only person
who would be my friend
at the time
when I needed one more than ever.
No questions asked, he was there for me.
It was the hardest year of my life and
he gave me good reason to smile,
a reason to feel good
when the rest of my world
was a place of darkness.

LAST WEEKEND

Friday night I was walking home past a bar.
A ball of flesh rolled out,
fists and feet sticking out like spines,
spanking out sounds like boat paddles slapping water:
Four guys were fighting,
eight others trying to pry them apart.
When the cops arrested someone, he said,
"Really, I've never even seen his girlfriend before..."

Saturday I was at a party
when two guys no one knew
showed up just to fight.
They had to be removed by force.

Sunday I got off work,
bought a bottle of wine,
and went to a friend's house and drank it.

It was a beautiful day.
My nose was not broken
and I was not in jail.

GOOD AMPHETAMINES, YOU KNOW WHAT THEY'RE LIKE

Well, I had seen them
read about them
been told about them
but I didn't know what they were like
so I tried them.

The first time it was like
coming down from Mt. Sinai with my face glowing,
It was like
finding a twenty dollar bill while doing my laundry,
It was like
well, you know what it was like.

So I did it again,
it was like
seeing the Virgin Mary,
it was like
finding a ten dollar bill while doing my laundry,
it was like
well, you know what it was like.

So I kept doing it until
it was like
being a priest with Turret's syndrome,
it was like
paying with a ten you thought was a one,
it was like
well, you know what it was like.

So I quit.
But it came around again,
a kind I had never tried before.

So I did it,
and I was on Mt. Sinai again,
and I was finding twenty dollar bills again,
but I knew what was coming,
and that it was going to come more quickly this time.
So I quit.

Now I drink way too much strong coffee.
You may ask what the difference is.
It's like keeping a muzzle on a pit bull,
well, you know what it's like.

MAGIC MARKER EPITAPH

I walked to the back of the almost empty late night bus
It was just me and the driver like a priest in a lonely cathedral

I read the graffiti multicolored
like stained glass all around me

Epic boasts and signatures
a history of the kids who sit on the back of the bus
and act as if they are scared of nothing

But the writing that caught my eye
was not a tag
it was an epitaph
scrawled in sad magic marker:

HP killed my nigga Peter Lee

For a moment
I felt like I knew Peter Lee and his friends
because we are all tied to the tracks
although none of us knows the order we are in

I pretend that this doesn't bother me
but it horrifies me
so I live my life like I am on the back of the bus
acting tough when I am really scared
walking alone on the sidewalk
looking in the mirror
or lying awake at night
waiting for the moon to come crashing through my window

Other people had gotten on
we had a moment of silence
bowed heads
It was probably exhaustion but I like to think otherwise

When I got off the bus
There was a man on the corner
blowing the blues with his sax
coincidental like a bad movie
I tossed him my change and walked home

Play on bluesman
Play on for Peter Lee
Play on for the rest of us because we're next
The tracks are vibrating
and the moon looks a little closer all the time

RUNNING THE GAUNTLET

2:30 a.m.
I was running the gauntlet
past the projects.

At the end of the first block,
a guy came up the street and said,
"Ten shot? Weed? Anything you need?"
"No," I said.
Two blocks to go.

A van pulled up.
"Hey, you got a smoke?" the man asked.
I gave him one, lit him up.
"You need a ride?" he asked.
"No," I said.
One block to go.

The van, going the other way, did a U turn,
and pulled up slowly.

I've been paranoid of this scene
ever since that night in L.A.'s Hoover District
when I was waiting for a near-mythical bus
and a low rider drove past,
backed up to where I was,
and stared at me with tinted window eyes.
I thought I was going to be shot
but they just drove away.

I started looking for cover when a voice
from the passenger side said,
"Hey, you got a cigarette for me, too?"

I gave her one with my matches.
I just wanted to be home.
"Are you sure you don't need a ride?
We're trying to get some gas money."
"I'm sure," I said.
They drove away.

I got home.
My roommate's bird was perched in the living room.
The cage is left open often
so she can fly around the apartment.
I went over to her,
she crawled onto my finger,
and I put her in the cage.
I closed the door
and covered the cage with a blanket.
She squawked.
"You're welcome, Percy," I said,
"Good night."

People have tried to sell me many things
but most of the time
all I want is a cage
and someone who will cover me like a blanket.

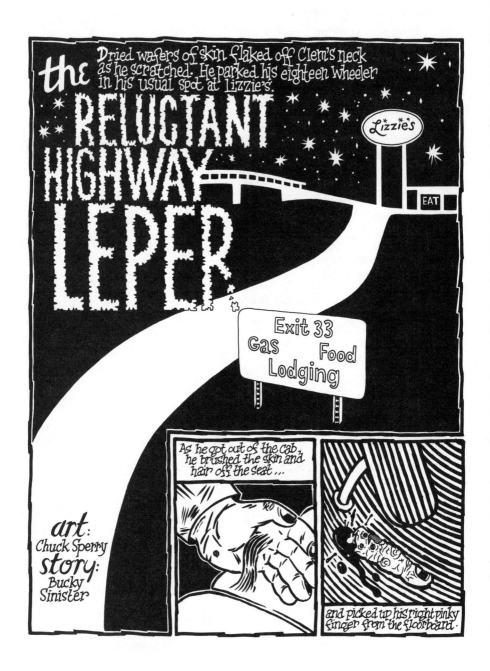

Aaw, nuts. It's a long story. I need a cup of joe.

Big Lizzie poured him a cup.

Thanks, he took a sip. Aahhh, well, all of you know how hard it's getting on independents.

Each trucker grunted.

So anyway, I get real desperate, and I take this under-the-table job with a load of toxic waste. I pick up in Rhode Island, and drive to New Mex.

The dump there got busted by the Feds by the time I got there, so I head to this place I know over by San Antonio. They won't take it neither.

CONDEMNED BY ORDER STATE OF ENERGY

So then, I try to get a hold of the boys in Rhode Island, but they tell me it's my problem, and they won't do nothing to help.

Phone Phone

Meanwhile, I start coughing up this black phlegm and throwing up a lot. So I start to thinking that maybe it's got something to do with my load, so I go back and open up. I see all them oil drums leaking something that looks and smells like Satan's afterbirth and I heave again.

Wuck

DO NOT OPEN
POISON VERY BAD

So I keep getting leaky on places, just wanting to get rid of it all, not wanting to leave the trailer somewhere. I been on the road for two weeks, now, darn near all my hair's fallen out, lost a lotta weight and most recently, I got some kind of weird leprosy stuff going on...

JOLIET MAXWEDGE

Joliet's left hand held the steering wheel. His right hand was clenched tightly around the grip of his .38 revolver named after Ringo Starr. He had his four guns with him that day, all named for the most famous British invaders. Joliet picked out the billboard advertising a German-made car. He stuck Ringo out the window and fired, putting a hole between the umlaut dots.

Joliet tossed the empty Ringo onto the floorboard and picked up George Harrison from the seat. Joliet flicked off the safety and looked for targets for George's fifteen bullets. Anything unAmerican would do, but pinko commies were preferred.

Joliet laid George in his lap and tilted the rear view mirror. He caught a view of his brother, Quentin, consummating his marriage with the newest member of the Maxwedge family. Joliet turned up the AM oldies station, but it couldn't drown out the sound of sweaty-flesh-on-carseat squeakings.

"Great balls of fire!" Joliet screamed along with the song. "Couldn't wait to get to the truckstop, couldja, little brother?"

Quentin did not answer. He was aware of nothing outside of the world of wedding cake aftertaste, backseat vinyl, and Penelope.

The good times were rolling, and Joliet was not going to be left out. His left knee came up for the steering wheel. Little Richard came out singing, Joliet's left hand strangling for that high note. George Harrison was in Joliet's right hand. Joliet's eyes fought between picking out targets and watching Lucille's sister doing what Lucille never would in the backseat.

The road bullwhipped under the whitewalls, and in Joliet's mind, it was 1959 again. 1959 was not only a good year, but the last good year and Joliet would hurt anyone who tried to convince him of anything different. The fifties were the days when America was number one and the Commies weren't welcome. Real cars were made for real men, like Joliet's 1959 Cadillac, people got married and had families like decent people should, and rock and roll was still music. Joliet knew he had been born a little too late. Back then things were better and he would've liked it and things would've stayed rosy forever but four Brits from Liverpool messed everything up. If they had just kept to their side of the ocean none of this would've happened and Joliet knew it was up to him to rid the country of all traces of them and bring truth, justice, and the American way back into style.

And what better way to clean up the squalor than with some hot and smoking American lead spitters? No Lugers or Uzis for Joliet. He held, by what he knew as his God-ordained country-given right to keep, bear, and use at will, American arms.

George Harrison was staring straight at a billboard for Japanese stereo products when Little Richard finally hit that drawn out high note. Joliet went cross-eyed, and fired off George. He doubled over with a jerk, his head hitting the steering wheel and knocking his knee loose. In a high-note haze, Joliet had visions of every hippie, commie, and other evil type drowning in an apple pie the size of Wrigley Field. The Cadillac swerved and 1959 disintegrated with a thumping jolt.

Joliet's head shot up and his right foot instinctively slammed the brake. The tires screeched, the newlyweds screamed, and Joliet ground his teeth to the Harmony of Prewreck. The car stopped by the shoulder.

Joliet got out of the car, zipped up his pants, and stuffed George Harrison in his cummerbund. He checked the front of his car. There was a little blood, but nothing that couldn't be washed off. Another good reason not to drive a tin foil import. American steel at its most purposeful.

Joliet heard his new sister-in-law crying as he went back to see what he had hit, praying with fervor that he had gotten lucky with a hitchhiking pinko. He came to a matted fur and bloody whimpering lump on the side of the road. It had been a dog once, and worse than that, it had been pregnant until the tire-tread miscarriage. It would only live a few more agonizing hours. Joliet took George Harrison and pointed him at the once-dog's head. George ended its misery.

Joliet was about to walk back to the car when he noticed the fetal pups. There were six two-headed pink closed-eyed unborns with their mouths open like burning witches calling to the devil. They were all dead, but an anger churned inside Joliet. Normal American dogs only have one head. Joliet went to all the heads and shot them off. Twelve shots later, everything was so quiet you could've heard a flag burning. Joliet had one bullet left and a bad ringing in his ears. He walked back to the car.

The styrofoam ice chest in the front seat chirped as he opened it. In the back seat, the dazed couple calmed one another. Joliet handed them each a can of Blatz beer and took one for himself and went out to sit on the hood for a little while.

The metal was too hot to sit on. Sweat had given Joliet's baby blue tuxedo navy patches. He sat on the shoulder with his head against one fender and rubbed the ice-water cold aluminum can against his forehead. When he pulled it down, he noticed he was bleeding a trickle. He popped the ring and took the first half of the can like a deep inhale. Dion cried to him from the car as he shot the girl on an import beer ad in her perfect teeth.

The nagging idea of having killed a mother was going to make the last leg of the trip to the truckstop a long one, but at least he had saved the country from six freaks.

Craig never should've looked in the trunk of the car. More than that he never should've looked in the plastic bucket that he found in there. All he had to do was drive. That was it. He wasn't paid to look in the trunk, wasn't paid to open up the bucket and find out he had been the courier for a severed head the last three hundred miles.

The job had seemed so easy at first. Just drive one of Mr. Digwell's cars out to Arkansas, pick up a package, and drive it back to San Francisco.

Do a good job, get the package delivered home safely, and you get fifteen hundred bucks and your immense debt with Mr. Digwell is considered paid in full as well. Fuck up this job, and we'll stick your legs in Mr. Digwell's piranha tank until you die. Craig still remembered Mr. Digwell's stout lackey's instructions verbatim.

Craig naturally assumed it was a drug delivery. After all, that's how he racked up a ridiculous debt to Mr. Digwell in the first place. He had just gotten too curious about what kind of drugs he was transporting.

Even if it had been just a head, he might've been able to deal with it. But it wasn't a normal human head at that. It was the head of a young woman with three eyes. That third eye wouldn't quit staring at him. His whole way out to the truckstop, she was staring through the trunk, through the backseat, right at the back of his head. Now she was staring at him in line for service.

The car just seemed to quit right by the exit. Craig knew no more about cars than he knew why he was delivering someone's head instead of drugs. Everything just blinked out at once. He had never had one of the cars break down on him like that.

The cars were lined up in front of the service station like sinners standing before God and it was taking so long Craig felt like he was behind the entire Nazi party of all history, getting their misdoings read off a list by the Almighty. The lanky bucktoothed Saint Peter read off broken parts like earthly misdoings sometimes just shaking his head condemning car owners to the Helliday Inn.

Craig took a quick survey of the surroundings. Two gas stations, a twenty-dollar-a-night chain motel, and a Darky's Rib Hut joined with a souvenir shop.

Darky's Rib Hut? Craig wondered to himself. Weren't they all shut down sometime right after the civil rights movement? He hadn't seen one since his childhood, but there it was, in full Stars and Bars glory hidden away right off Highway 98. It had been at least twenty-five years since he'd seen the ten foot tall statue of LeRoy, the plump and smiling pickaninny mascot, frozen all this time in a running position, holding a plate of barbecue ribs in one hand over his head.

"Buds?"

A voice interrupted his thoughts. Craig looked down at a Deadhead kid who looked a lot like the auto mechanic.

"Do you want any buds?" he repeated. "I got the kind."

Craig opened his mouth and realized he'd been chewing his lip raw. "Uh, yeah, that sounds like a good idea."

"Hey, Coy, watch my friend's car," the kid yelled. The auto mechanic looked up, smiled, and winked.

Craig and the kid walked off around Darky's Rib Hut and sat by the dumpster.

"My name's Leonard, but you can call me Shadow Walker if you want," the kid said, trying to sound mysterious.

"You sure my car will be okay?" Craig squinted into the distance.

"Yeah, Coy, the attendant, he's my cousin. My friend's going to be coming around the corner with some happy grass. He's cool, just don't say nothing about his face."

A rough-skinned, sinewy man around six feet tall but looking like he only weighed 120 pounds came around the corner. Craig noticed he had no cheekbones.

"Hey, Highway. Have a seat."

Highway sat down next to Craig and pulled a joint out of his shirt pocket. He fired it up, took a hit, and handed it to Craig. Craig inhaled and handed it to Leonard. Leonard took a drag and handed it back to Highway.

The longer Craig held in the pot smoke, the more he could feel that three-eyed girl's head staring at him from the car. He blew out the smoke in a coughing fit.

"Good stuff, huh?" Leonard's buckteeth grinned at him. "Want more?"

Craig shook his head no. Getting more paranoid was not what he needed now.

"My name is Highway 98..." the strange-faced one droned.

"Highway's got the gift of sight," Leonard interjected and babbled along with Highway.

"...and I was born when the first car crawled down that road..."

"This is what he always says before he prophesies," Leonard said, with anticipation in his voice.

"A queen will find a king, bards will sing of lead, and over a woman someone will be dead."

"Though you never know exactly when it will happen even if you figure out what the heck he's talking about," Leonard added, and then changed the subject. "Hey, you ever been to San Francisco?"

Craig started to speak and felt like he might have never really been stoned before. "Yeah... that's where... yeah, um... I'm headed... uhhh... was, I mean..."

"No fucking way! I've never been there! Can you take me with you?" Leonard was practically squealing.

"Car fucked," Craig managed.

"I'll find you a ride, man, if you'll show me around there," Leonard promised.

"Uhhh...sure..."

Leonard jumped up. Craig was amazed at how this kid could move like that after the pot. He looked to his left. Highway was gone, replaced by a pregnant dog. Craig jolted. The dog was sniffing around. Leonard waved for him to follow. Craig hypnotically stood and started to walk.

The world went by Craig as he stayed in the same spot. A seat in Darky's Rib Hut slid underneath him and he sat down. The waitresses looked like Leonard. That confused him so he looked out the window. The pregnant dog was there. He thought it was white and brown before and now it was black or another dog or something and that confused him. He turned back around and stared at the swirl of Leonard's shirt.

"Hey," Leonard yelled, "anyone give me a ride to San Francisco?"

A man in a baby blue tuxedo turned on his stool to face Leonard. Craig had to remind himself he was stoned, because the man had daisies around his head and his skin was green, and when he opened his mouth, Craig saw sharp points.

"Hey, Judester!" the man said. "Put some flowers in your hair, you just got yourself a ride."

Craig sat on the bucket with the three-eyed girl's head in it underneath the shade of the Darky's Rib Hut awning. Dawn had snuck up on him, and he still felt like he was a little stoned. That had been no ordinary pot, Craig thought. Whole families were checking out of hotel rooms and coming in for the Wham-Bam Breakfast before they hit the road. Craig hoped he would soon be in San Francisco.

A family gathered by the door. Craig heard a little girl scream and start to cry, and the family went inside. A boy who appeared to be nine or ten was left there with a puppy.

"Hey kid, let me see what you got," Craig said. He thought the boy looked a lot like Leonard.

The kid came closer. He had a two-headed puppy in his arms. "My name's Simon. This here is Lucas and Marcus. What's your name?"

"Holy shit..." Craig muttered.

"Your mama must not've liked kids," he said with a bucktoothed grin.

"Craig, my name's Craig... where did you get this dog?"

"Pretty weird, huh? Only one from his litter to live. Strange, usually it's a female that's the strongest as pups. He's not for sale."

"Nah, I don't want it, I just wanted to look."

"Yeah, everyone does. Don't it just beat all?"

Craig's response was cut short by a stare coming right up through the bucket into his ass. Leonard walked up with a duffel bag. Highway 98 was walking a bit behind.

"Hey, Simon, your mama's looking for you," Leonard yelled.

The kid dropped the puppy and ran off, the puppy following behind.

"See ya met my cousin Simon," Leonard sneered.

"You got a lot of family here?"

"Yeah, a little too much. So hey, this Joliet guy is supposed to be here any minute now. What's in that bucket?"

"Uh, well..." Craig was interrupted by Joliet's Cadillac screeching in front of them. The top was down and the radio was blaring the Big Bopper.

"YOU KNOW WHAT I LIKE! You boys ready?" Joliet got out of the car and opened the trunk. "Gimme your stuff and I'll put it in the trunk. Go ahead and take your seats, the flight to Frisco leaves soon."

Leonard threw his duffel bag to Joliet. Joliet put it in the trunk. Craig picked up his bucket and took it over.

"The hell's this?" Joliet said.

"It's a mummy's head for the San Francisco Museum. Very important."

"Oh. Whatever. Wanna beer?" Joliet threw Craig a beer. "Get in up front."

Craig sat down in the front passenger seat.

Joliet sat down in the driver's seat. He looked in the back at Highway and then back to Leonard.

"I AIN'T TAKING NO MONGOLOID INJUN FOR NO RIDE!"

"Shut the fuck up, man, we're the ones paying you," Leonard retorted. "Do you want our money or not?"

Joliet stared awhile, then turned back around. "Okay," he muttered. "But he doesn't get any beer."

Joliet put the car in drive and took off. The day kept getting hotter and Craig was still too stoned to speak much. He kept trying to decide if he was still high or not, even though he knew it was too long to still be stoned. The high came and left in waves.

The high was creeping up on Craig around noon. He took his shirt off. Chuck Berry was on the radio.

"MAAAAAAAYYBEEEEEEEELIIIAINE!" Joliet screamed. Craig thought he sounded nothing like Chuck Berry. "Hot enough for ya, Cowboy?" He looked over at Craig. Craig wanted to hide inside his beer can, but just took a slug instead.

"This highway here is the old highway from before they built Highway 98. Nobody takes it anymore so the cops don't even bother coming out here. You can go as fast as you want and nobody will give you shit.

"Take a look back there. Hippie boy and the retard redskin are zonked out. Probably fags with each other," Joliet sneered. "So. Anyway. How much you willing to sell that girl's head to me for?"

Craig looked away. "You mean mummy's head." Craig started to hear a whine, like a baby's whine. He wasn't sure if it was the pot or the car.

"Mummy's head, my ass. I got ulcers older than that three-eyed girl. I don't know what you're doing with it, but I bet the police sure would like to know. "

"Hey... I don't know what I'm doing with it either," Craig said defensively, the whine increasing. "All I know is that I'm being paid fifteen hundred bucks to deliver it to San Francisco."

"Balls... Fire!!! For fifteen hundred she'd better be the fucking Queen of England."

Joliet pulled over into an abandoned Darky's Rib Hut. There was still a statue of LeRoy smiling, cracked and paintchipped in front of the building.

"Piss break." Joliet got out of the car and walked around the building. The whining was still getting louder. He knew he wasn't just imagining things. It was coming from somewhere.

Craig walked over to the collapsing roadside artifact to get a better look. All the windows were broken out. Inside was a room-sized salad made of dry leaves and trash, with beer cans sprinkled on top like croutons. Still the whining continued, but it had been louder by the car.

The pot kicked back in. Craig forgot where he was. The entire time between the truckstop and now had been clipped out of his memory. Hadn't there been people inside just a moment ago? How many Rib Huts have I seen? Just one or two? Am I high now, or am I sober and able to realize what is really going on, so the other people, that whole truckstop, was a hallucination? Thoughts and doubts raced and careened through Craig's mind like a paranoid pinball, until he heard the trunk slam shut.

Craig's first fear was for the head. He turned around to see Joliet pulling something out of the trunk, but he couldn't tell what it was. Leonard walked around the corner, zipping up his pants, looking down. The whining was now a scream. A baby's scream, like some kind of ever-hungry spawn crying for its demon mother's breast. What if that sound is something that I can only hear when I'm high? Craig thought. Joliet raised a shotgun, aimed for Leonard, yelled, "Hey Judester!" and shot twice. Dark red holes, each a lip-flapping mouth screaming in pain, opened up on Leonard's tie-dye shirt as he jumped backward, flipped over, and landed dead on his stomach. Joliet walked to the frozen Craig. He pointed the shotgun at him.

"Don't wet your pants, cowboy," Joliet sneered. "I let the retard get away, why not you too? Remember, I coulda killed you and if you feel like coming after me, I will. I figure a guy like you is in too much trouble with the law to go to them for help. But I don't have anywheres near fifteen hundred bucks and I gotta have that head."

Joliet held the barrel a foot away from Craig's chest. Craig saw the word *John* written on the barrel with a magic marker.

Joliet backed up to the car and opened the trunk, keeping an eye on Craig. He put John in the trunk and pulled out Paul, since he could hold it in one hand. He picked up Craig's bucket with his free hand, took it to the backseat, and opened the lid. Then he went to the glove compartment and opened it up. The whining became a full scream. Craig realized this was where the screaming had been coming from the whole time, something in that car had been wailing and crying this whole way. Craig just couldn't hear it until he got stoned on that weird weed. He saw Joliet wincing in ear-shattering pain and knew Joliet could hear it, too. Joliet pulled something out of the glove compartment and held it over the open bucket. It was a tiny human skull, jawbone still attached but totally slack, screaming in full horror and pain.

"I now pronounce you man and wife," Joliet screamed over the sounds of his dead youngest brother shrieking away. "Kiss the fucking bride!"

He dropped the skull into the bucket, and suddenly, Craig heard no more screaming. Joliet put the lid back on the bucket, shot the statue of LeRoy in the teeth, and took off down the highway.

Everything sounded so quiet to Craig. Something cold and wet touched Craig's hand. He screamed. He looked down to see a pregnant dog licking his hand.

Joliet's left hand held the steering wheel. His right hand was gripped tightly around Paul McCartney. Joliet picked out a billboard advertising a Korean-made car. He fired, put the gun in the passenger seat, and tilted the rearview mirror to take a look at his youngest brother and the newest member of the Maxwedge family consummating their marriage in the bucket.

I WAS WITH HER LONG ENOUGH TO CHANGE
BRANDS OF CIGARETTES

We had split a bottle of wine and a pint of rum
before we went into the fair.
It started with a kiss on the ferris wheel.
I didn't know that actually happened until then.
One of my favorite days of all time...

Six months later
I gave her money that she referred to as "fetus money."
We were long over as a romantic couple.
That day she listed why she hated me.

I had told her that I was sorry and I said so again
but those words can't take away a clumsy fuck.

The way she talked to me
it sounded like her mistakes
never hurt anyone but herself.
My mistakes have bad aim
and always seem to hit those near me.

She looked so young
I felt so old
I had driven another away
or she'd changed
or vice versa
whatever it was
it was done
and I was tired of looking.

SHHHLINK

They called white boys "warm up drills"
(White boys were known not to want to play
    basketball for money)

Phil and I went to the parks
    looking to pick up two on two half court games

Basketball music at the time
was Whodini or Midnight Star

We shot over a blasting
Five Minutes of Funk
and Phil would pick up a game for us

Ten-to-win
make it, take it
and no blood, no foul

They would almost always
let us have it first
I would check the ball and
predictably
my man would back off
give me room
and without moving either foot
I'd put one up from twenty feet

SHHHLINK

Phil and I had met a few months before
Both part of the same cause
he had been assigned to me to

personally monitor my spiritual growth
He brought a ball to our first meeting
said I would learn how to
play basketball for Jesus
I told him I was too slow
too clumsy to play
and he said
"Have faith, little brother"

There was no "swish" on those courts
The nets were made out of chain links
and they made a "shhhlink" sound

After the first shot
they'd give the ball back to me
and the question always was
"Yeah, but can you do that again?"

SHHHLINK

Phil had played NCAA Division III ball
before dropping out of school
to work for the ministry full time
He taught me how to shoot and rebound
against taller and faster opponents

Phil would check it the next time
fake a shot
beat his man
my man would run
to guard him
leaving me open
bounce pass
two feet from the basket

SHHHLINK

About this time the other teams
would actually start to play us
with their friends heckling them from the side
"Damn, you letting some white-ass motherfuckers beat you"
We would still have the ball
and sometimes score two more
before they could get it back

I saw Phil about four or five times a week
Most of the time was in a more directly
Bible study group related place
but the courts was where we became close

Time slows down
as you get higher in the air
until at the peak of your jump
time stops
you release the ball
your ears deaf to the music
gravity, slowly and gently
lowers you down to the ground
heads all look up
the ball spinning backwards

The ripping of a clean shot
was all the trash talk I ever needed

After the game was over
Phil would pitch his evangelical bible talks
which made sense enough to them to listen
because how else could a couple of dorky white guys
walk onto their court

give them a beating
their friends would never quit talking about
without Divine help?
Yeah, they could buy that

Phil and I played together for a year
After a while
other regulars at the Framingham courts
would hustle other players and put money on us
with generous odds
We made a few people rich
plenty of people angry
and even got a few of them into Bible studies
but they rarely ever kept coming

Phil got assigned to monitor someone else
and then I only saw him about twice a week
and neither of us really had the time to play together after that

Sometime in the next year
I realized the nets
weren't the only ones wearing chains
and I made a fast break from Boston

I played a few pickup games in college
but they
had never heard of "make it, take it"
they kept score by twos
had glass backboards
called fouls
no music
and worst of all
rope nets
It just wasn't fun anymore

Now
when someone gets on the bus
and drops twenty nickels in the hopper
I think of those nets
ripping in slow sound motion
I think of Phil
who I haven't talked to since leaving the group

When I have good dreams
my legs are stronger than they ever were
and I'm right in front of the basket
I jump
higher than I ever have
and the chain net comes closer and closer
my outstretched right hand has the ball
When time stops
my hand
ball attached
is just above the rim
I dunk
and hear
a slow echoing SHHHLINK

WHEREVER YOU ARE

I would write you a letter
but I don't know where you are anymore.

For years you have kept in touch
with a mutual friend
only under a vow
that he would not reveal this information.

He slipped up the other night and said
the two of you had talked.
He was the one who
four years ago
told me you were married
and supposedly that was the last
anyone had heard of you.

He kept your secret
wouldn't even give me your new last name
only told me
your child's name
wouldn't even tell me why.

I can only think of the nights we spent together
how I revealed my past to you
the one I used to lie about to others
how I clung to you
when the nightmares were at their most frequent
and I saw the world through
fear-colored glasses.

I don't know who you married.
Maybe a man

with flaccid emotion
who never cried with you
but just held you instead.
Maybe a man
with no sexual wounds
that got in the way of intimacy.
Maybe a man
who sleeps upon desire
for as long as he wants
and never wakes up
grabbing you
not recognizing you
or the room he's in

I don't blame you
if that's what you always wanted
because I can't give you those things

By now
your name
your location
even if you still love me
doesn't really matter
if you don't want to be near me
but the one thing I still want to know is
when your child screams at night
do you think of me?

LOVE, SPILLING OUT ON THE FLOOR

I woke up on the tracks
(you were tying me down)
your screams like vultures
circled over my head:
"You treat me like a whore!"

But you:
you treat me like a john
you
a prostitute with a purse full of masks.
When I met you the mask was unconditional love
but you don't wear that one anymore.

What we had together
spilled out onto the floor
left a stain shaped like a gut pile
and now it rots in the carpet.

I take the empty vessel
and inhale the fumes:
Hot rails and rope burn
Love and nausea
Herbal tea and hatred
Blood and a breakfast cigarette

I am a drowning man
strangling on the rescue rope
I am a mother in denial
and the wetnurse suckling her dead child
I am an accident victim
and the motorist running over the severed limbs
he reaches for.

And like an old man
who refuses to remove his broken watch
I can't ask you to leave me
but I hope you will go on your own
because I don't have the time
to love you anymore.

THE CRIME OF DOGMA

It doesn't matter what you believe
It doesn't matter how strongly you believe it
all that matters is
will it hold your mind together?

Do you remember when you believed
in the infallibility of adulthood?
    Indian head test pattern breakfast
    monochrome mantra
    sitting too close
        because no one had figured out
        your eyes were bad yet?

Do you remember
    the burning of the gravel
        in your hands
    up and under your skin

    becoming airborne over the handlebars
    too far from home
        and you can't get the chain back on?

Do you remember
    that first time out at church camp

    "Have you ever been to the cross?
    Seen a man hanging in pain?
    Seen the look of love in his eyes?
    Then I say you've seen…"

    Crying children
        smelling of Deep Woods Off

listening to the story
of the kid who got baptized
at camp last year
and when he got home
he got hit by a car
and he's in heaven now
and when you leave camp and go home
and get hit by a car
where will you go?

It's time to put away childish things
It could happen to you
like a thief in the night
it could happen to you
like a thief in the night
the LORD comes
and what will you say
when you stand before him
on the day of reckoning?
Like a thief in the night
your innocence and carefree nature
were taken away
replaced by a mission
a goal for the Kingdom of God
your assignment given to you.

Do you remember the water
cold salvation
creeping up and around you
buried in the blood of the lamb
rising from the water a new life ahead
a new creation
a blessing in the eyes of the LORD?

Do you remember pulling the wings off flies?

And when the call came
you were there to answer
    "Here am I, LORD, send me
    out into the fields
    where the harvest is plenty
    but the workers few..."

Do you remember believing
    knowing so strongly
    no one could tell you different
    feeling on fire with the true path
        I am the way, the truth and the life
        no man comes to the father
        except through me
    the only way to enlightenment, empowerment, and salvation?

You told everyone you could
the knowledge of your correctness
giving you the courage
    to confront, disarm, and win over
    unbelieving hearts and minds
changing lives and psyches around you

Do you remember
    screaming how right you were
    the veins in your neck and head
        like binding rope
    your frightened heart
        trying to escape your chest
    concealing your shaking hands?
    It was an uphill battle
        you were only too glad to fight.

Do you remember
    the catchphrases, the slogans, the buzzwords

you wore like armor
and wielded like a sword

the all-night work parties
fueled with enthusiasm and self-righteousness
giving up sleep, food, and time
for something you thought was more important?

you felt power
you felt secure
you felt so vital to the way of truth.

Someone stole it while you were sleeping
your head was turned
or you weren't paying attention
you're not sure who or when
but somewhere in all the confusion
you lost your stable footing
     your peace of mind
the fervor and zeal replaced
with fear and doubt.

Do you remember a shaken belief
     an impurity in the faith
     the words of other ways making sense
     feeling burnt out
     wanting to get off the path
     feeling bewildered, weakened, and damned?

You felt like no one could understand
     how lost you were.
So afraid to look for help
     you looked around and all you saw
     were hearts and minds mutated
     by the radiation of your dogma:

horrible phrase spouting monsters
spitting sincere babble like blood.
They frightened you so much
you didn't dare scream
at the smallest sign of weakness
they would've torn you apart
ground your bones to make their bread
lathered themselves in your fluids
decorated themselves with your entrails
like one of Hell's Christmas trees
you fooled them only long enough to run.

During the day you run
at night their hounds come closer
their howlings the soundtracks for your nightmares.

One mistake later
and a lifetime to regret it:
I now know
one mistake is all it takes
to make sleep an act of bravery.

Should've known better
Should've known not to play
three card messiah at the crossroads
Should've known
when you play the Jesus
the devil comes up.

What are we to do now?
Now that we are home from the war
and all we know how to do is
kill for Jesus
how to take apart and reassemble a Bible in the dark
and how to speak in collages of rhetoric?

All I can do now is wait.
Closing my eyes
I can feel the wet foxhole around me.

We thought that by
    clinging to a philosophy
    by embracing an ideal
    by holding fast to the dogma
we were somehow empowering ourselves
but all we ever empowered
    was the dogma itself
and when it dropped us
and we shattered on the floor
    like a wineglass dropped in shock
we were left drowning in an ocean of fear
struggling to grab hold of anything
that would hold our minds together.

We only wanted to save people's souls
and if that took
wrecking their lives
rewiring their heads
we did it
because to us
the ends justified the means
and we needed the eternal soul profit
we made from corporeal raiding.

But the means got meaner and meaner
and the sake of the means
    became the ends
and the greed of evangelical recruitment
took us over
until it was as if
we were only recruiting
so we could have more people recruiting.

The wingless flies are laughing
at the freshly amputated
limbless children
bleeding and writhing
on the cafeteria lunch tables.
It's not karma.
It's payback.
The stench from the rotting appendage pile
snakes into the noses of the squirming tortured
like a memory of the
innocence they had when they did the act
they're paying for now
but they can't get that innocence back
any more than they can
pick up their legs without any arms.

As the judge in the courtroom of guilt, regret, and fear
slams down his headache gavel
I dedicate this testimony:
this is for everyone who knows
        revolution
        is not a political slogan
this is for everyone who knows
        revolution
        is not a burning cop car
this is for everyone who knows
        revolution
        is not mutilation.

And in this time
when it is so easy to find a revolution to die for
I dare you
find a revolution that will die for you.

PEGBOARD

I drink to get the nails out of my head. That's the only reason. I hate other drunk people. I swallow past the taste because it's medicine that I need. On the days the nails are hammered past my eyeballs, alcohol keeps me stable.

I've had headaches for years. Constant headaches, all day long. Doctors always tell me it's psychosomatic, related to my trauma, so instead of prescribing some kind of migraine medication, they want to put me on psychoactive drugs. I'd rather have nature's stress and trauma remedy: alcohol. So when I need a break from the pain, I just pop into a local beer clinic.

My bar at one time was Patrick's, a sports bar. It was decorated with antique and vintage sports equipment. I had been heavily into sports at one point in my life, and Patrick's reminded me of the time before my life got so out of hand. The regulars there left me alone. That was exactly what I wanted. The only time they ever spoke to me was about the pegboard.

The pegboard was up on the wall, an old board from an ancient Phys Ed class, worn wood with two vertical rows of holes made for climbing. A pegboard works like this: stick two pegs in the board and lift yourself up chin-high, take one wooden peg out and stick it into the next hole, and repeat the process until you're at the top two holes. The holes are evenly spaced, but each level up seems twice as high as the last.

I happened to hold the pegboard record, and occasionally won myself drinks by demonstrating my talent. It was rare to find someone else in the bar who could make it all the way to the top, and even then, no one was faster than me. When I wasn't climbing, I was just another sports oddity gargoyled over my drink.

I had gotten a good start on relieving the tension of one nail that was coming through my right cheekbone, one nail throbbing in the base of my skull, and another protruding just below my hairline in the center of my forehead while watching the Red Sox game on the television, when I heard the words.

"Hey, faggot," a slurred voice said. Somehow I knew this was aimed at me. Call it spider sense, ESP, or macho meter, but sometimes you just know without even looking who they're talking about.

I didn't turn around. There are three steps to getting a man to fight. He had just committed the first by attacking my sexuality. The game was close with the tying run on third, and I didn't count that as an insult anyway. I knew what this guy wanted, and I wasn't about to give it to him.

"Hey, motherfucker, I'm talking to you," the same voice said as a finger thumped my shoulder.

Step Two is saying something mean about my mother. This was not original at all, but it was close enough to count. Even if I had known my mother, there were two strikes on the batter. The Red Sox were having a good year for once, and I wanted to see every win I could this season.

A stubby-fingered hand spun me around. Damn those swiveling barstools. The hand was connected to an aging onetime high school football hero. The index sausage poked my chest. Step Three: annoying physical contact.

"Hey, dickhead, I'm going to take your girlfriend home tonight, so if you got a problem with it, I oughta kick your ass now," he said, as if proud of being able to form an entire sentence. I didn't have a girlfriend. I had no idea who the hell he was talking about. I stared at him, amazed at his stupidity. I turned the stool back towards the television.

The pitcher released the ball as I was spun back around and punched in the right cheekbone. Immediately, the right half of my face numbed. This was the effect I was paying for.

I looked at the frustrated ex-jock. I saw him as if he were on a martial arts chart, diagrammed for strike areas of the body. There were arrows at his nose, neck, groin, and knees. He looked so ridiculous this way I snickered.

"What the hell you laughing at, sicko?" he screamed, spitting.

My face was cut. I didn't know until I felt something running down my lip, licked it away and tasted that salty-metallic taste. Blood.

Still, I couldn't get angry enough at the guy to care about hitting him back. He had a dopey looking Brian Bosworth haircut, short on top, long in the back, with lines shaved into the sides of his head, and way too much gel spiking the top up. His face was red and it looked like it was puffing up. This guy looked so ridiculous I laughed out loud.

"What are you, some kind of pervert?" he sputtered with a crackle in his voice. He just didn't know what to think about a guy who gets insulted, threatened, and punched and just laughs in return. "Keep your goddamned bitch!" he screamed, and hurried out of the bar.

I looked back up at the game. There was a commercial on. I had missed the crucial pitch.

"Pegboard! I mean Allan, whatever," Nicole shrieked, running up to me. She was a regular like myself, but we didn't know each other too well. "I'm so sorry. That was all my fault."

I was confused. "What are you talking about?"

"That guy was hitting on me so I told him you were my boyfriend so he would leave me alone. I had no idea he would do that."

I felt another trickle and wiped my shirtsleeve across my cheek.

"Hey, it's all right, I guess, you know, cause he's gone. That's what's important," I said, glancing down at the smear on my shirt.

"But you're hurt!" she said, grabbing a napkin and pressing it to my face.

"Buy me a drink and we're even."

"Okay, sure," she giggled, probably surprised I was taking it all so lightly.

She bought me three Bass ales, actually, in the next hour and a half. As my buzz grew, the coldness of the steel in my face lessened. We both got drunk and talked about the Red Sox's chances for winning the pennant.

When the game ended, the Red Sox choking again, she got a concerned look on her face. "That cut won't stop bleeding and it looks like your eye might swell. Why don't you come over to my place and I'll clean it up?"

We had been drinking, and I wanted to eliminate the possibility of anything happening between us. I knew I wouldn't be feeling anything until tomorrow anyway. "Nah, it's nothing, thanks anyway."

"No, it's no problem. Really."

"I gotta get home soon," I lied, unable to think of a reason.

"Come on. I live on the next block. Please? It'd make me feel better."

"Okay, whatever."

She smiled and we went into the street.

"Peg—Allan—er, uh, what do you want me to call you?" she asked.

"Any Bosox fan can call me Allan."

"Thanks," she giggled. "Anyway, I don't want to intrude, but I've always been curious about your limp," she asked nervously.

"What about it?" I said, annoyed.

"So, is it true? Did you get hurt in the Colts' training camp? I mean, Dick told me, and he knows everything about everyone at Patrick's."

What a bunch of crap that was. Dick was not only a bartender at Patrick's, he was also a champion bullshitter.

"No, but I did hurt it my last year of high school football," I was lying but she wouldn't have believed the truth anyway. I wouldn't either, if not for the scars. It's so fucking surreal, I wouldn't even know where to begin. There are always those moments of your life that people say they want to hear about, but as soon as you tell them, they start treating you different. Either you've freaked them out or they feel so sad for you nothing will be the same.

Nicole mentioned something about wanting to be quarterback of the football team when she was in high school, she had some kind of incredible passing arm, but I missed the rest of the anecdote because I was looking at the hardware store on the corner. I started wondering if I would still have my headaches after I sobered up, when she stopped by a door.

"This is it," she chirped. I followed her back to the living room. There was a sliding glass door leading to a back porch. "Have a seat. I'll get something for your cut."

I went to her video shelf. Mostly sports related: Doug Flutie's Boston College vs. Miami game, career retrospectives of Yaz and Ted Williams, and too many '80s Celtic games to count. I pulled a videotape off the shelf. It was marked *1986 Baseball Highlights*.

She came back into the room with a bottle and a washcloth.

"Can we watch this?" I held up the video, hoping she hadn't seen it too many times.

"Yeah," she smiled. "But only if you take this like a little soldier. Sit down."

I sat down on a comfortably ragged sofa to take the hydrogen peroxide. She tilted the bottle, holding the washcloth under the cut. I felt the tingling burn in my cheek and took a quick breath. Nicole wiped my face. Some of the blood had smeared into a pale brown by my ear.

She put the videotape on, but when it played, it was a soap opera. "What the hell?" she shrieked. "Angie, you bitch!"

"What? Who's Angie?"

"Angie's my roommate. She tapes her soaps while she's at work. I'll rip her throat out! I was lucky enough to see the Red Sox make it to the World Series once in my lifetime and I want the tape to prove it!"

I started to mention that she had forgotten about '75, but caught myself before I did. She was probably three or four years old back then. I had been finishing up high school at the start of that season.

"Aw, hell," I said, "We probably know every inning of that season anyway. Hey, can we go out on the porch?"

"Sure," she muttered. It sounded like she was going to be pissed about this one for a while.

When we came into the house, it had been light outside, but now it seemed almost completely dark. From the light coming through the sliding glass door, I could see that the deck wood was new.

"Nice deck."

"Thanks. Our landlord's brother is redoing the whole thing. The old boards were rotten for a long time."

"He's doing a fine job," I stated, admiring a job well done.

"You know much about woodworking?" she asked, a bit surprised.

"I was into carpentry once, sort of," I said, and the "sort of" kept it from being a complete lie. I hate lying to people but I always get too intense of a reaction from the truth. This was the best time I'd had with a woman in years, even though we weren't doing much of anything. I didn't want to wreck the whole mood with some what-fucked-up-my-life story. For a moment, I looked into the sky, wondering what the stars would be like if they were in a perfect grid pattern. Then I realized the nails were back, even though I wasn't completely sober.

Nicole sneaked up in front of me and poked me in the chest. I looked down and she kissed me, almost missing my lips. I looked at her and realized I was extremely attracted to her. I must've seen her in the bar for the better part of a year, but had never exchanged more than a quick hello and goodbye, or how-bout-that-game kind of talk.

We kissed again, part of me wanting to for hormonal reasons, and the other part wanting to be distracted from the mounting pain. My sex drive had just come out of hibernation.

"Allan," she said, looking up. I wondered how I looked on a background of stars. I could imagine light shining through me. "Let's go back inside."

She took my hand and led me to her room. Then she started kissing me with violent search-and-destroy kisses. I was feeling euphoria from her and pain from myself, so I wasn't even aware when she pulled off my shirt. Then she saw the scars.

"Holy mother of god! Allan, what the hell happened to you? I'm sorry, I mean, are you okay? Well of course you're okay, but I'm a fucking idiot..."

I've got a perfect grid pattern of scars on my chest, legs, and arms. It's all part of my past that's so hard to describe. They are actually old nail holes.

"Shhh. Stop it. It's okay. Really, I'm used to it. Everyone freaks out when they look. Even doctors wince. Why don't we just turn out the lights so you don't have to see?"

She smiled an apologetic smile and turned off the lights. I stood still in the darkness and let her come back to me. One hand found my chest, shaking a bit, and the other followed. They persuaded me down toward the bed.

I lay down, and Nicole sat right above my crotch. I reached up to pull her to me, but she took my wrists and put them down under her knees. I had no idea what she was doing. I didn't know how to react so I just let her do what she was going to do.

Her hands moved across my chest, down to my stomach, then up my chest to my arms, across to my shoulders, to my chest, in that pattern, again and again. It was sort of like a massage, only more caressing. My eyes had adjusted to the darkness, but I closed them anyway.

As I fell into the rhythm of the pattern, her hands stopped feeling like hands. Instead, it felt as if I were becoming aware of certain points on my body and they were warming and contracting.

I started to breathe like I do before an anxiety attack, and I could feel the oxygen in my blood. I saw swirls of purples and greens. Then I felt the nails in my head heat up. The burning was a searing electrical current, like the nails had been hooked up to a power source. Then they moved. The nails were moving out of my head. Not that I couldn't feel them, but they were leaving, slowly pushing their way to the surface.

Tiny nails, numerous as hair, were the first to go. Due to the other large ones, I had no idea that they were even in there. It sounded like a box full of bottles dropping off a roof. If my pains were rooted in tangible sources, her floor would've been covered with metal debris. Then the large ones said their final goodbyes.

With the last three clunks of steel hitting hardwood, the room was so quiet. I could only hear my ears ringing and her hands moving across my skin. I also heard a whimpering and realized that it was me.

My body was shaking as I opened my eyes. It looked almost like daytime. Nicole was the physical manifestation of beauty. I loved the smell of stale beer, I loved the taste of the air, and for the first time, I felt the ability to really fall in love. The glass walls separating me from life had shattered and the possibilities really were endless like I had always heard. Everything was beautiful and lovable, I was alive again, I was feeling like I felt before all that bullshit with the bed of nails. I had been sure there was no way back, not ever...

"Allan, what's the matter? Why are you crying?"

"You just put the blue back in the sky," I said, the tears coming steadily. Fuck, that sounds stupid, I thought, but I was too overwhelmed to think of anything else.

"Thanks, I guess," she smirked.

I pulled my hands out from under her knees and grabbed her shoulders with them. She came down to me and I kissed her with trembling lips. We made love after that, but that part is all just a blur now. That night I dreamt not of steel and wood, struggle and pain, but of serenity.

Over the next two weeks, we saw a lot of each other. We would meet at Patrick's and then go to her place. We planned a trip across the country to Fenway Park for next season, or that season if the Bosox went to the World Series.

Finally I understood what the whole fuss was about sex. For the first time, I was experiencing a healthy sexual relationship. It was purely carnal and enjoyable, no more overtones of fear and pain.

I quit drinking so much, since whenever I felt the nails, I went to her. The relief still came, but not as intense as the first time. Still, I thought there was hope that she would be some kind of savior. Somehow Nicole would help me end this pain-filled part of my life.

My dream states had calmed down dramatically since that first night with her. One night they unfortunately went back to normal and the nightmares returned in full force.

That night I dreamed of the group from my past again. I still hadn't found the courage to explain to Nicole who they were and what they had done to me. I was afraid of wrecking what little relationship we had, I didn't want to take the chance that she would leave me if she knew everything.

In '79 I joined a sect of renegade physical fitness freaks who could be best described as Buddhist monks and S/M enthusiasts. The group learned everything we could about our bodies, wanting to push them to the most extreme point possible without dying. Our ultimate idea was to get ourselves to the verge of death, and sustain it for as long as possible, overpowering corporeal shutdown through sheer will.

We came damn close with one particular method. We found a way to insert nails straight through a person into a board underneath without killing them if they were properly trained with the right yoga and meditation techniques. I was one of the first to try it, and the only one who lived long enough to give it up.

The dream picture was so precise. I tilted my head up and looked down at my body, or what I called my body then.

The smooth plywood underneath me, the twelve-inch nails in a two-inch grid pattern pinning me to it, the I.V. solutions flowing into veins almost running on top of my sunken skin, the gray masonry block walls, all crystal clear as I watched a cockroach crawl up onto the top of a rib, its antennae waving at me. I tried to move and felt the stinging sears of the nails all over. I kept trying to count them, but I couldn't even see them all. One of the initiates came into the room and flicked on the light. I would've closed my eyes, but I had overcome the trivialness of retinal pain at this point. The cockroach ran in the valley between my ribs and underneath me, where it was probably feasting and laying eggs. The initiate had a sponge and a bowl of water. He began to wipe my bald head.

"Sir, if only I had faith such as you, I would be whole," he said, in an emotionally rushed and trembling voice.

"How are my brothers?" I wheezed.

"Uncle Andrew's faith proved incomplete last night."

My brother Andrew had let me down as well as himself.

"How has your sleep been?" he said, changing the subject.

"I had this strange dream..." I started, and then realized that I was still dreaming, and that I had to wake up right away. I tried screaming and thrashing about, but I couldn't move, I was nailed solidly, and the pain traveled up and down my body.

"No, my uncle! Be strong! Have faith!" shrieked the initiate.

I woke up then, my right arm underneath Nicole. I jerked it free.

"Rallrun," she muttered and fell back to sleep.

I sat up and stared at her, three headaches poking deeply in. I wouldn't be sleeping again for a while. It amazed me how other people slept, hours and hours in a row.

I slept a combined two or three hours that night and woke up to a gloomy sunny Saturday. Nicole woke up slowly and cheerily. I was on the porch drinking coffee when she put her arms around my neck and kissed me. I jerked.

"Morning, sweetie. Jumpy already? Must be some good coffee," she cracked.

"There's more in the kitchen," I said, and she disappeared.

I thought then about telling her my story. I knew that soon she would think that she understood me well enough to hear it, but I didn't want to scare her off. It's so rare that I can meet someone I don't want to ignore.

Nicole came back with a cup of coffee and the morning paper and started reading sports scores. I looked at the coffee can of nails and the hammer that had been left on the porch and somewhere in the National League roundup the whole picture went out of focus and the nails in my head were like icicles.

That night we were on her floor together. I was in pain, trying not to think, just to feel her body move under and around mine, but I couldn't stop.

"Oh yeah," she wailed.

The floor was cool and hard. A firm wood. There were still nails and a hammer right outside. It would be easy, I thought. I was much stronger than her, and after the first few, the rest would be no problem. I was more turned on than I had ever been. That is what I wanted. That is what I knew I needed. With each stroke in, I was hammering another nail. With each stroke out, I was lifting high and aiming.

"Oh Jesus, yes!"

I could feel her quaking as she came. I thought my abdominal muscles would rip away when I came. I collapsed on top of her.

"Al-lan. The way you do me, oh God!"

We crawled into bed. She kissed me a few times on my chest, then curled up into me and fell asleep. I wanted to go home, but I felt like I was stuck.

That night I dreamed of being an initiate again and coming to her with a sponge and a bowl of water. I didn't wake up frightened. I woke up ejaculating. It was crumbling again. That whole time in my life was still directly wired to my sexual drive. Somehow my whole mind got fucked up back then. Acts that repulse me mentally appeal to me carnally. I'm not sure I'll ever be able to have a long term sexual relationship with anyone.

What do you say love is? Is it fair to tell someone you love them just because it doesn't hurt you to fuck them? Should you say you love them when it's gratitude for an absence of pain? Sooner or later sex starts to hurt again and I always feel like moving on.

Nicole worked on Sunday mornings. That next morning, when I woke up for what I decided would be the final time with her, I was alone. I decided to walk down the street to find some late breakfast.

On my way out, steel started coming into my head like I was a pin cushion. I walked by the hardware store. It had just opened. My breathing got heavy, and my adrenaline pumped. My vision was a bit wavy. I walked to the bins.

I put my hands on the side of a bin of long headless nails. The metal smell went straight to my legs, which started to quiver. There was not enough air in the store, but I was unable to walk outside. I leaned on the bin with my right arm and picked up a shaky handful of nails with my left. After looking at them for a while, I pressed them to my face. They were cool like a breeze on a misplaced kiss. I took a final breath and blacked out.

I woke up looking into the face of a paramedic. I had fallen backwards and gotten a bad cut on the back of my head, and bled a large puddle on the floor. They took me to get stitches.

When I got home, I unplugged my phone. Nicole didn't know where I lived or worked. For a month I avoided her and the rest of what I was forced to claim as reality.

After that time passed, I decided I had been too callous to her. I had no plans of getting back together, but I thought I should go apologize.

I called her, but no one answered her phone, so I headed down to Patrick's. Ted was bartending.

"Hey, Ted," I said, like I had seen him every day.

"Hey, Pegboard! Haven't seen you in a long time. What's going on?"

"Been real busy. You know how it is. Hey, Nicole around?"

"Not today. She's been looking for you. She's moving to Boston. I know you guys had some kind of thing going on, so maybe this ain't cool to bring up, but she met some benchwarmer for the Red Sox straight out of Pawtucket and now she's going out with him."

"Sounds like she's doing okay." I shrugged, and parked myself at the bar.

"Yeah, who knows?"

Dick came over, pudgy faced and drunk, and slapped me on the shoulder. "Pegboard, man, long time no see."

"Yeah, I been busy."

"Hey, know how it goes. Look, man, there's some tourist kid from England here, and when I saw you come in, I told him how fast you can do the board, and he bet me twenty bucks you couldn't. Ten's yours if you can. Whaddya say?"

Ted was paying full attention.

"Ted, get the pegs," I said.

Ted handed me the pegs and I went up to the board. Dick picked me up and lifted me high enough for the first two holes.

"Peg-board, Peg-board," the bar chanted.

I hadn't done it in a long time. I went over and up, up and over. My shoulders, elbows, and wrists were made of fire. The pain glowed at each old nail hole.

"PEG-BOARD, PEG-BOARD!"

One hole to the next, up and over. In hole. Out hole. Over. In hole. Out hole. Up. The next hole is all there is. I create it going in and destroy it coming out. Up on the board, I am god.

NIGHT OF HORROR AT QUICKIE MART

We stood over the body, quiet at first, like the humid summer woods around us. The pine trees stood towering and reverent, the only mourners the dead girl had. It was the middle of an Arkansas July and a sour milk smell overpowered all the other forest scents.

Her hands and head had been cut off so we didn't know who she was. She looked young, no more than a teenager: no stretch marks, wrinkles, or that kind of thing. Since she was cut up like that, we figured she had been murdered. We agreed to keep it a secret from everyone but the sheriff so maybe we could collect some reward money, but first we had to get the corpse into town.

Dale, acting like the deer hunter he is, picked her up and put her on the hood of the truck, I guess as a joke, but who knows. He was dumb enough not to know any better.

Roy came around to the front. He slugged Dale hard in the arm. "Dale, I swear you're too stupid to be my brother. Put her in the bed with Jimbo and Greg." Dale laughed quietly, scooped her up, and put her sprawling in the bed.

Great, I thought, I gotta ride in the back with Jimbo again. Jimbo and I climbed into the flatbed, right behind the window. We scooted her as far away from us as we could with our feet. As we got on the dirt road that left the woods, I looked at the leaves stuck all over her naked body like handprints, and I wondered what her face had looked like.

Highways feel so smooth compared to dirt roads; it feels like you're flying. The way Roy drives, all he would need is a pair of wings anyway. After the pickup hit the highway, we were back at Jimbo's house in no time at all.

Roy and Dale got out of the truck. "We can take the body back into town," Roy stated with authority, "since we're going that way and all. Me and Dale were talking about it, and we think it'd be better if we didn't take her back in the open bed, so we were wanting to use your Chevelle."

"Well, I guess," Jimbo said, sounding reluctant, digging in his pockets for his keys. "Bring it back tomorrow and we'll switch back."

"Great," Roy said. Jimbo tossed him the car keys. Dale and Roy put the girl in the trunk and took off, spewing gravel from Jimbo's driveway.

Jimbo got into the cab of the truck to give me a ride home. "Damn it!" Jimbo barked, and slammed his palms on the steering wheel. "Hey, Greg, looks like you're staying over tonight. That dipstick Roy done forgot to give me the keys."

I looked over to where his mom's stationwagon was. It was up on blocks. There was only one other car there, a rusting Camaro Jimbo was trying to fix up. It had been there since last year but he still hadn't gotten it running yet. I followed Jimbo into the house, trying to figure who had the better deal, myself or the girl who got to ride in the trunk of the car. Jimbo's the kind of guy you don't mind doing things with, but you don't want to stay at his house.

I came through the door, and a stench hit me that made me wanna puke.

"Jimbo, did you fart?" I asked accusingly, waving my hand in the air.

"Nope," he denied. "What's for dinner, Ma?"

"Hog's brain with cheese, green beans, and fried okra," replied a voice from the kitchen.

No wonder it smelled. These people were bonafide country hicks. Don't get me wrong, I like food like that, but whenever you eat with people like this, you never know what part of the pig you're really going to be eating.

"Jimbo, I think I'm a little sick from looking at that girl," I lied, holding my stomach.

"Fine, go back and lay down in my room if you want," he said, grinning, probably thinking about what a sissy I was.

After supper, we were out on the front porch sharing a cigarette. A pair of headlights with a truck attached turned off the highway and came down the drive. Jimbo blew out some smoke. "Looks like Matt's home," he said, pointing at the jacked-up four wheel drive.

Matt turned off the engine and limped past us, not saying a word as he went into the house. No way was I gonna ask him for a ride home. Matt made Jimbo look normal. Jimbo was just a little confused because his family was inbred a little. I give him room to be a bit strange since he is his own uncle. But Matt, he's just plain looney.

We were still talking about half an hour later when Matt came out to join us. I tried to make myself as invisible as possible.

"How's it going, Matt?" Jimbo asked, handing him a cigarette.

Matt lit himself up. "Got fired again. Some college boy from State came in and tried to buy a case of beer. I carded him and wouldn't sell to him, so he flipped me off and I had to beat the daylights out of him. Eugene, that pimply little dickhead, got all excited when the guy's nose was bleeding everywhere and Eugene thinking he's such a bigshot since he's the manager and all, decided to fire me right there. 'Don't get mad at me,' I says, 'cause I ain't the one bleeding all over the damn place,' but he just kept yelling, 'Get out, get out.' "

"You didn't need that job anyway," Jimbo said.

"Hell if I didn't. I've gotten fired from just about everywhere in the county."

We didn't say nothing else until Matt finished his cigarette and the two of us went inside.

"Matt hasn't been able to get a decent job ever since the state fired him," Jimbo informed me.

"What'd they fire him for?" I asked. I figured maybe he'd killed somebody, although I probably would've heard about it if he had.

"Okay, well, it all goes back to when he was driving those monster trucks a couple of years ago. You remember that?"

"Yeah," I said. Matt had gotten a DWI right before the big King Of

The Mudpits show at the Coliseum and was barred for life from competition.

"Well," Jimbo continued, "he really misses that action. Still is all he talks about. His favorite part was working on them big engines. You know, him and one other guy built the entire engine for Chief Clobber Claw. Anyway, for his community service, he went to work as a scab to replace the striking highway workers. He still had his operator's license, so they put him to running the steamroller. One day, the steamroller shows up missing. They asked him where it was, and he told them he lost it. 'How the hell do you lose a steamroller?' they ask, and Matt says, 'I don't know, I just lost it, it won't happen again.' They said, 'Damn right it ain't gonna happen again, cause you ain't gonna be working here no more.' So after that, they set him to picking up trash on the side of the highways. Word got around, and now no one wants him. All think he's gonna rob 'em blind. Enough to drive him crazy. The only thing that's kept him sane is that project he keeps working on in the old barn. Won't even tell me what it is. Just keeps saying that when it's done, his problems will be over. That should be any day now from what he says."

"What do you think it is?" I asked.

"Best guess is a hot rod he'll take around to car shows."

Jimbo got up and went inside. I followed him in, and that night I tried to sleep with one eye open.

We called up Roy and Dale the next day. Their mama answered.

"Hello," her voice sang. Her name was Dovey. She had the voice and disposition of a dove, and the body of a prize bull.

"Hi, Mrs. Baker, this is Jimbo. Can I talk to Roy?"

"Nope. Sorry. Roy and Dale are grounded," she lilted, hiding both anger and disappointment.

"What's going on, Mrs. Baker?" Jimbo winced. He hoped she hadn't gone near the trunk.

"Well, I'm sorry to have to tell you this, and I'm sure you know nothing about it, you being such a good boy and all, but they were hiding a bottle of Jack Daniel's under the porch and sneaking down there and drinking it."

"Now, Mrs. Baker," Jimbo sweet-talked, "stop kidding with me. I know Roy and Dale would never do such a thing."

"Believe me, I was just as surprised as you are. I didn't raise them in my Christian household to act that way," she warbled.

"Well, that's too bad. Even the runner stumbles."

I didn't know what Jimbo was talking about at the time, but the way he talks to someone's parents always makes me laugh. When he wants to, he can speak completely in phrases from Christian inspirational greeting cards.

"Could I just talk to Roy a bit? He's got my car and I got his truck but I don't have his keys."

"We noticed they didn't come home in the truck and we thought that was your car. Their father can bring you the keys this afternoon since he's going out that way anyway. You can't talk to them, though. Their father caught them red-handed drinking on that whiskey under the porch. They were too scared to come out and their father was not about to spend all day crawling around after them, so he got some two-by-fours and nailed them up in there. We'll let 'em out tomorrow if they're ready."

"Well, you have Roy call me when he gets out. I'd appreciate it," Jimbo said with an extra helping of fake gratitude.

"Will do, Jimbo. Take care," she crooned.

"You too, Mrs. Baker, bye-bye." Jimbo hung up and when he told me what happened, I laughed so hard I almost took a leak in my pants.

It was Friday night and me and Jimbo were leaving Roy and Dale's house in Jimbo's Chevelle. Jimbo'd brought a sack with him with half a watermelon, a bunch of yarn, and a pair of old rotten work gloves. I asked him what it was for but all he would say was "Later." We agreed to take the girl in on Saturday, cause there was no way we were going to let this cut in on our prime cruising time. We got into town and cruised a little only no one was out yet so we went up to the Quickie Mart to hang for awhile.

We were the only ones in the parking lot. Jimbo and I got out.

"You go in there and distract Eugene," Jimbo said with a grin. "I've got a little joke to play."

I didn't know what it was he was talking about, but I figured as long as he's warning me, I'm not going to be the butt of it, so I did what he said. I went inside and started asking Eugene for cigarettes I knew they didn't have.

"Marlboro Menthol 100s in a box?" Eugene was puzzled. "You don't even smoke menthol, do you?"

"Heck yeah, I do. I bought them here yesterday while Matt was working. Could you look in the back for me?"

"Well, I guess. You keep an eye on things for me." Eugene went off into the back. I heard Jimbo slam his trunk shut. Eugene came back in.

"Don't have any of those. Knew we didn't," he said in a know-it-all voice.

"That's okay. Just get me a pack of Reds." I bought the smokes and went back out by Jimbo's car. He was laughing.

"Look in the back seat," he giggled.

I opened the back door. The smell hit me first. That girl had spent the whole two days of ninety degree heat, ninety percent humidity, in the trunk. She smelled worse than Death's armpit. Jimbo had put the gloves on her hands and the sack on her head.

"The watermelon half is her head and she's got some pretty yellow hair."

"What the hell is wrong with you, Jimbo?" I yelled. "This is the stupidest and sickest thing you've ever done!"

My mind went through the Jimbo's-fucked-up-ideas file. I'd known him as long as I could remember. When we were young, it was small things. Pulling the wings off flies, tying a string with a can on one end to a dog's tail, you know, mean but usual kid stuff. Then came thirteen or so and he never stopped. It just intensified. He spent all one day catching frogs and then spent the next day crucifying them down by the creek. He taped M-80s all over a stray cat and threw it into a trash fire. The cat ran out screaming, singed, and finally convulsing in death throes from the tiny but powerful explosions. Maybe I never noticed because this stuff all happened so gradually, but for some reason this was the first time I realized Jimbo had a serious problem. But what the hell are you supposed to do when you realize your best friend is a psycho bastard?

"Trust me," he said, grinning like a mad scientist. "It's the smartest thing, if not the craftiest."

About an hour and a half later, Lenny Stone pulled up in his El Camino. He got out and went into the store. In the passenger seat was none other than a very drunk Adam Green. Jimbo went over to the window and knocked. Adam rolled down the window. He was so wasted he could barely sit up.

"Hey Adam, I know something you want to know," Jimbo taunted.

"What?" he spat, his head lolling up to face Jimbo.

"We've got a girl passed out in our backseat. You want a turn?"

Adam was the most undersexed guy in the county. He fucked a chicken when he was fifteen and hadn't gotten laid since that we knew of. At least not with people. He should've just changed his name to 'The Guy Who Fucked A Chicken' because that was how everyone referred to him anyway. The chicken laid bloody eggs for a week and then died. Adam was pretty much branded on the forehead by the whole thing.

He opened the door and tried to get out, but the seatbelt was too much for him.

"C'mon, get me out," he slurred.

Jimbo undid the seatbelt and we helped him across the two parking spaces over to the Chevelle. Adam stank of sweat, whiskey, and vomit. He had dipstains from his Skoal all over his face. We opened the door, pulled the seat back, and shoved him into the back.

"She stinks!" he yelled.

"That's just her puke on the floor," Jimbo said. "You don't mind, do you?"

"Nah," he said, trying to get his pants down. "Lookit this bag. She must be a real dog, huh?"

Jimbo slammed the door shut. "We're going to give you two lovebirds a little privacy," he said, and we went inside. I was laughing so hard I cried. Lenny was inside at the counter. Me and Jimbo tried to let him in on the joke, but both of us were laughing so hard we couldn't catch our breath. We followed Lenny out to his car, laughing like loonies, and then we heard the sound from down the road.

It was a roar like an airplane engine. We all looked down the road and saw a steamroller careening towards at about ninety per. When it got closer, we saw that the driver was Matt. Everyone ran for it and hid behind the dumpster in the parking lot of the grocery store next door.

The steamroller was straight from the bowels of Hell. Flames were shooting out the back from some kind of turbine that looked like it came straight off an airplane. The thing was doing wheelies. Where there wasn't chrome pipes or tubes it was painted glossy black. It was headed for Quickie Mart, with Jimbo's Chevelle in the path.

The Chevelle was bouncing up and down and the windows were fogging up. I started to run back, but Jimbo grabbed my arm. There wouldn't be time to get Adam out.

The Steamroller from Hell went right over the Chevelle and crushed it instantly. Tires popped, glass crunched, and metal flattened. I kept telling myself that Adam was a jerk and he had it coming anyway, but no one needs to go out like that.

"Oops," Jimbo squeaked.

Matt drove right into Quickie Mart with his steamroller screaming like a dinosaur. He hit the fountain drinks, the snack aisle, the microwave oven and everything else, but saved the panicking Eugene for last.

A cop car pulled up right as he was leaving. Two cops with shotguns got out. Matt gave it the gas. The cops unloaded on him. Matt died with his foot on the gas pedal, and the steamroller was halfway over the cop car when his body fell off.

Lenny ran over to his car which had escaped damage somehow, and started kissing it.

"What now?" I asked.

"Aw, the cops will find Adam and the girl in the back, won't ever be able to tell that she was already dead, probably won't perform an autopsy or anything. The insurance on my car will give me enough to get the parts I need to get my Camaro running, and maybe even a paint job."

Jimbo and I just stood there for a moment, looking at the mess. The steamroller's front wheel was smeared with Twinkies, mayonnaise, Snickers bars, and the innards of three people. Two more cop cars came, along with paramedics and firemen. They took turns posing for pictures in front of the steamroller. With all the lights flashing, it looked like one heck of a party.

"C'mon," Jimbo said. "Let's see if Lenny will take us cruising."

We couldn't agree on who would sit in the back.

I LOVE U$_{238}$

Last night
while listening to Pachelbel's *Canon in D*
I dreamed that I was tied to a huge violin string.
The cable saw/piano wire hairs of the bow
were pulled across and into the trunk of my body.
My abdominal wall tightened up
but it didn't do much good.
I wanted to scream
but my diaphragm was being cut as well
and the blood ran down my chest
and around my neck.
The piece ended and I awoke.
I was balled up on my bed
with a severe stomach cramp
and Bach came through the speakers.
I got a vision of Shiva scratching a chalkboard
and decided to get out of there and go for a walk.

The guy at the corner said
"Anything you need?"

"Yeah," I said, "what about some happiness?"

"Forget it, man," he said
"They don't make that like they used to.
These days it's all cut with
materialism
and false hope.
But hey man
I can get you
depression by the gram
loneliness by the ounce

or anxiety by the pound."
I just walked on
the tumors of despair
swelling inside me.
I got this cancer from being too close to a pile of beauty.
That stuff is radioactive
don't let anyone tell you different.
It decays into cliché
like the song that decays into screeching
like the high that decays into addiction
and the sludgy wastes
they're always easier to obtain
like the ever abundant hatred
but they are toxins
that or the hunger for them
will kill us all one day.

THE TECHNICOLOR BLUES

Roy and I sit on the stoop.
His twelve bar blues
turn the street into a TV set.
Piece by piece
streets, fences, people, fire hydrants
it all turns into a cartoon.

Tex Avery hungry wolf crackheads
wanting money
settling for cigarettes
hide from Ralph Bakshi pigs
(now ain't that a switch).

Betty Boop/Popeye hipsters
tattoos in the spaces between piercings
mount and dismount motorcycles
looking for that perfect (check as many as apply):
___heroin   ___bad pizza   ___fashionable cigarette
___Seattle sound   ___import longneck   ___blurred sex experience
while it's still cool.

Kookoo for Cocoa Puff Tweety Birds
killing time between raves
with handfuls of abbreviated-letter drugs
they bought from Dr. Seuss
carry their Eye of the Storm nervous systems around
like crumpled out-of-date flyers
they don't bother removing from their pockets.

Walt Disney princesses singing
"Someday my credit rating will come"

and knights in designer armor
look straight ahead
as they head to a wannabeapub bar to throw darts.

Stragglers drawn to the guitar
leave the cartoon parade
and sit with us between frames.
They tell us their technicolor blues
and we hear the same stories again and again
like sound effects.

"I keep seeing this tunnel"
they say, and it's
the tunnel of (check as many as apply):
___love   ___cheap rent   ___financial stability
___fashionable vehicle   ___vice of choice
no matter who sits down and then
"But when I try to run through it
it's only a painted black half circle."

Then they leave
off to do their business
before Porky Pig
comes in his full rapture glory.

Roy and I sit on the stoop
steamrollers coming down the street
anvils and baby grand pianos falling from the sky
waiting for Natascha to walk by.

KING OF THE ROADKILLS

300 miles from home
going 75 miles per hour
in my mother's 1985 sky-blue Ford LTD
and I have a bad look in my eye;
I'm looking for the exit
that isn't there because I missed it.

I missed the last exit to peace of mind years ago
and at philosophical truck stops
    at religious gas stations
    and from schizophrenic state troopers
I get "You can't miss it" directions back to the highway
but I always end up lost...
Being lost is about trying to go
from point A
to point B
and ending up at an unexpected point C somewhere in-between.

I roll down the window
and spin the AM dial.
All I can think about
    as the preacher prays for me
All I can think about
    as people call in to the radio talk show
    worried about bad marriages
All I can think about
    as the preacher asks for my money
All I can think about
    as people call in to the radio talk show
    worried about
    rock and roll music, psychic vampires, and boll weevils

All I can think about
    as the preacher screams so loud
    the veins in his forehead must be sticking out
    like the road map that I need
All I can think about
    as the sky bubbles
    and the dead possums declare me King of the Roadkills
All I can think about is that point A and point B
are two shackles of different metals
that are choking me

and I'll settle for any point C I can find
as long as there's room to breathe.

DIVINE SYMPHONY OF THE DAMNED

Hard grind for a hard time
There's so much to feel
So little time

Pain don't mean nothing anymore
A laugh don't mean nothing anymore
Bodily functions don't mean nothing anymore
No regurgitation
No defecation
No pigeons pecking at your spit on a hot day
    and you can't figure out why you feel so cold

There's no time to figure out why
You've got little time to live
You've got little reason to live
You've got less reason to die

Reason doesn't mean anything
    when a madman plucks discordant strings
    and makes the world go round
The divine symphony of the damned plays on
    and there you are in the crescendo
The music your life makes
    is just another thing you hate
    that you have no power to change

The neighbors complain that the music's too loud
    but the volume knob is nowhere to be found
    and you have no time to look for it
    There's no time to learn the words
    no time no reason to play air guitar

with a razor blade
Just slam down that gas pedal and drive
Suffocate that gas pedal and drive

Put on Pink Floyd
    because it's just like you
Put on the White Album
    because it's just like you
Put on Black Flag
    because it's just like you
Put on Skinny Puppy
    because it's just like you
Steve Albini is your mother singing you to sleep
    when a rubber room devil is laughing in your ear

You can scream as loud as clenched teeth will allow
    but it won't take the white from your knuckles
    or the red wildness out of your eyes
You can scream as loud as clenched teeth will allow
but it won't make your drugs work any better
    it won't make anyone love you
    it won't make your prayers reach the ears of your gods
You can scream as loud as clenched teeth will allow
and you can kick your head back
    and open your mouth as wide as you can
    let your screams explode out
    and travel to the sun to be swallowed
    and then you'll discover that
    you will need another mouth or two
    to scream as loud as you want
So what's the point?
No reason to scream
No time to learn to scream louder

But look for the guy by the side of the road
with no arms and no legs
hitchhiking with his tongue—
that will be me
Stop, pick me up, give me a ride
and together we will scream loud enough
    to make the wind stop blowing
Together we will scream
    the music we cannot get away from
Together we will scream
    the blue right out of the sky
And when the brakes go out at the top of the hill
    it will be all you can do to steer

REDLINING WITH ETHYL

Wheeler's fingers ached for Ethyl's strong flippers. He impatiently stared up at her from his skate wheel platform. He watched her caress the faces of the others with her soft red lights.

"Oooh, the bonus is lit, go for the bonus, handsome," Ethyl teased. Her voice echoed in the expansive warehouse.

Wheeler looked at the legs of the other three. Legs were all he wanted, all he needed to be able to look down into Ethyl's table as the others were playing. Gazing into the plastic over her scoreboard was the best he could do.

The four around Ethyl were like obedient schoolboys, never speaking, only listening, snakecharmed by her flirtations. They waited anxiously for her to speak the same way a prisoner in the hole waits for his meal. They were so enthralled, they didn't hear Luthor and Eric come up behind them with a five-foot nitrous oxide tank.

"Hey, you rattle-hungry rags, we scored, so form a line," Luthor yelled with a laugh.

Wheeler's head popped around in unison with the others. The ball drained down Ethyl's middle. Wheeler reached into his jacket pocket. Trembling fingers found his flexitube and whipped it out. As he screwed one end into his nosevalve, he looked back at Ethyl. He felt like a whore. His hunger for the gas was taking him away from her. Ethyl reflected his look.

"Next player, take me now," Ethyl moaned. Wheeler looked back at the tank, pretending to have forgotten he was next. The skin on his neck and cheeks became warm.

"Eric and I hit first," Luthor ordered. "Small hits. We've got plenty of gas and time for redlines later."

Wheeler watched enviously as Eric screwed his flexitube into the valve on the tank. Eric put one hand on his nosevalve and the other on the tank to steady himself. Luthor turned the faucet. Eric tucked his chin and squinted his eyes shut. The flexitube jerked and stiffened. Wheeler felt like a starved predator when he heard Eric's artificial respiratory system give a loud whirring noise as he inhaled. Blood began slamming through his veins and arteries. He closed his eyes and whiteknuckled his hands around the edges of his platform. When Wheeler heard a squeak from the faucet being turned back, he opened his eyes. Luthor unhooked Eric's flexitube and attached his own. Eric's eyes snapped open with a laugh and an intense but quick shake of his head which left his flexitube dangling wildly.

"That Jack," Eric yelled, "always scores us the cleanest rattle!" and he turned the faucet for Luthor. Wheeler shut his eyes again, squeezing the edges of his platform with impatience, wanting to tear something with his hands. He wanted to mangle, to rip and claw something apart, to cause something to feel the pain he lived in. He listened as Luthor took his hit and unhooked with a raspy laugh. Luthor went over to Ethyl.

Wheeler scooted up next to the tank and Eric hooked him up. It had been almost two days since he or the others had sucked any amp-gas at all. The flesh around his artificial parts was aching. The metal in his body felt as if it were spreading, trying to poke its fingers into what was left of him. His veins were sore. He hadn't eaten in that same amount of time and the taste of his metal teeth was playing mind games with him; the aftertaste was enough to make him want to rip his tongue out. His thoughts were of blood, burning gas fumes, oil slicks, and gunshots. When Wheeler could sleep, he dreamed gun metal and napalm dreams. No one cared. No one noticed. No one except Ethyl. She talked him to sleep. She calmed his schizophrenic anxiety. She alone kept him from going over the edge.

Eric turned the faucet. The gas inflated his windpipe to full capacity. Wheeler's respiratory system cycled faster and faster until it hit three times its normal speed. The gas was coming to him as if he had extra lungs running on a perpetual inhale. Strength filled the veins of his arms. His halfplastic heart pumped with enthusiasm. The colors around him started glowing. Eric shut off the faucet.

Wheeler unhooked himself and went to join Luthor at Ethyl. His old prosthetics, clumsy and worn out, felt new. The mimicking hollowness was gone. At this peak, he could not remember the pains he felt only minutes ago.

Wheeler squeaked over, wrapped one arm around one of Ethyl's front legs, and leaned on her. He looked up at the engrossed Luthor. "How does it feel getting beaten by a legless man every day of your life?"

Luthor laughed. "Not as bad as it feels when it takes a day and a half to score some decent rattle. Unhook the chainsaw from my belt, willya?"

Wheeler unhooked the blood-covered butcher's chainsaw from Luthor's belt, picked up a rag from the floor, and started to wipe it clean. Luthor continued with a snicker.

"So for a day and a half, me and Eric was lurking around everywhere from the financial district to the pleasure strip, and it was picked clean. By this morning we was looking for anything. There was nothing. Not a rag lying in the alley, much less anything slightly human, nothing. So we gave up and decided to come back out here for help, when there on the catwalks in the industrial zone, some rag-brained fool was walking alone with two healthy, pink flesh, muscle, bone, artery and vein legs like something out of a redline hallucination! So Eric and I realize that it was real, and the next thing you know, raghead's on blocks and we're down at Jack's scoring the biggest rattle tank we've seen in months!"

"Oooh, extra ball," Ethyl whined as Wheeler and Luthor cackled over the story.

"Can't say I don't know how the guy feels," Wheeler said, breaking his laughter and putting down the chainsaw. He remembered the buckshot raining through his body, the taste of his own blood in his mouth, and the smell of burning flesh. In his next conscious moment, he had stumps for legs. "What's Jack been up to?"

"Not much, besides the usual, you know, trading body parts for rattle and motorcycle parts and working on his bikes. Oh, yeah, he told me something kinda weird... C'mon, Ethyl, baby! Don't drain me... That's it... Yeah, so anyway, this kid comes into his bike shop, marked up like a common music rag, listening to Bullet Mob or something on his radio, with his hair rigged and everything. This kid says he wants to score a three-hit rattle tank. Well Jack knows that this kid could score for almost free down at the clubs on the pleasure strip, he's got the look and all, so he knew something was polluted here. He sells the kid a tank, but filled with carbon monoxide, the kid hooks and hits hard, trying to redline, his eyes roll back and he falls on the floor. Jack drags him into the back to strip and freeze him and would you believe the rag had holotattoos of Sewer Crew on his chest and back? He finds a map on the kid leading to here... C'mon Ethyl! Don't treat me like this..."

The ball drained despite Luthor's intense shaking.

"Same player, shoot again," Ethyl pleaded. Luthor pulled back on the plunger and let it go. Ethyl squealed.

"I can't believe those rags are still trying to junk us," Wheeler laughed. "Hey, what about the stripping? The guy's legs, I mean?"

"I asked him about that... yarrgh... C'mon, Ethyl... And he said they would be too small for your height and weight. They were standard mech pros, so it's doubtful he'd be able to trade for something in your size. You're a..."

"Yeah, I know, hard guy to fit."

"Ethylethylethyl! Nonononono!"

The ball bounced indecisively and went down Ethyl's left side. Luthor picked up Wheeler and sat him in the hammock-like harness so he could play. Wheeler pulled the plunger back and sent the ball into play. Ethyl gave her familiar squeal. His hands fit over her corners, his fingers rested lightly on her flippers.

The two were quiet for a moment. In between Ethyl's noises, all they heard was pressurized-gas-released squeaks and laughter.

"Luthor, homeboy," Wheeler said seriously. "You notice anything strange about the others?"

"Like who?"

"All of them. Take a look at Gator."

"Something strange with Gator? No fucking way," Luthor said

sarcastically. He looked over to the group sitting around the tank. Gator was unhooking and smiling with his jagged lips. He returned Luthor's gaze.

"No, there's something polluted," Wheeler said. "When was the last time he talked?"

"I haven't been taking notes. What's up?"

"It's been at least two weeks. But that's not all. No one else besides you and Eric and myself has said a word in the last three days. Just that stupid rattle laughter. The last time Michael spoke he mentioned the black clinic off the pleasure strip."

"The one where we traded some of our body parts straight for rattle?" Luthor asked.

"The same one. Look at them. Junk that, look at us. We've gotten most of our pros in the last two years. I don't mean our resp systems, that was survival, but the rest of it, the second-rate rigwork. The legs you have. That voicer of yours. When you talk you sound like you're sucking glass."

Luthor winced. "Hey, we would've lost the legs in this part of town anyway, and my voicer just needs a little work."

"Hey, look, homeboy, all I'm saying is at this rate, we'll be all metal, fiberglass, and plastic in no time."

"And?"

Wheeler himself didn't understand why he was so bothered. The crowd around the tank was still hitting and laughing. Only Ethyl could think of anything to say.

"The bonus light is lit. Go for the bonus, big boy."

"Junk this noise. I'm going for another hit," Luthor said, and left Wheeler alone with Ethyl. Wheeler picked up the bonus with a deft flipper shot.

Ethyl and Wheeler were two ballet dancers harmonizing their bodies together. Ethyl lit her targets and Wheeler guided the ball to them. No one was able to do the things to her that he could. No one could make her feel the way he did. He knew exactly how to shake her and never tilted. The silver ball was in complete submission. Gravity had no power over love.

Luthor yelled over to Wheeler. "Hey, Wheeler, you want another hit?"

"Yeah, bring it over."

Luthor and Eric brought the tank over. Luthor looked at Wheeler's score.

"First ball and you're already about to put the high score even further out of our reach." Luthor was in awe.

Wheeler caught the ball on the left flipper. Luthor held it for him. He didn't want to take his hands away any more than he would've wanted them cut off, but he knew it wouldn't be long. His hands came away from Ethyl slowly. His palms were moist. He looked at his reflection in Ethyl's window plastic and gave a wink. He hooked up and Eric stood ready at the faucet.

"Let me redline," Wheeler said, and Eric twisted the faucet. Luthor and Eric watched him closely, afraid of accidentally killing him by breaking his respiratory system.

Wheeler was still feeling the effects of the first hit, and this one hit with even more force. He could hear his respiratory system cycle faster and faster, until it was just a whirring whine in his brain. He could hear something like angry chimes sounding in his head. He could feel the parts of him that were artificial, as if they were separated from his natural parts: the respiratory system in his chest, the metal in his face, and his halfplastic intestines and heart. The tubes in his throat were like hot snakes wrapping around themselves down to his fake lungs. The metal in his face felt like it was merely resting upon his skin. His stomach sat majestically on his intestines. Then his whole body melted away, except for his bones which felt like they were rattling. Then they disintegrated into a forgotten moment, and Wheeler was in a wind tunnel, he was falling from a building, he was a highway with motorcycles crashing on him, he was nowhere at all...

"Shut it off, Eric! He's redlined already!" Luthor yelped. Eric turned the gas off. Wheeler's body slumped into the harness, and the two waited for him to revive.

Wheeler's consciousness came back to his body, and he felt the expected euphoria. The colors around him intensified. His body felt like one piece again. Through a haze he gave a rattlegrin. Luthor and Eric laughed and unhooked him. His head lolled around at will. Wheeler shook his head quickly and resumed his game with Ethyl.

"Look, Wheeler," Luthor said, "we want to crash the pleasure strip since we're all revved but I'll stay here with you if you want."

"Nah, man, go ahead."

"You sure?"

"Yeah. Say hi to Jack for me and bring me back a pizza. I'm starving."

"You gonna be okay here alone?"

"Who's alone? I've got Ethyl to keep me company."

"All right, see ya later."

"Don't forget the pizza, and no black olives or I'll break your neck."

"Sure thing, homeboy," Luthor yelled on his way out. The others were already out of sight.

"Yeah, keep it turned. Hey, it probably won't even be your ball by the time you get back," Wheeler yelled but Luthor was too far gone to hear him.

Wheeler caught the ball on his flipper and gave Ethyl a scan. She burned erotic casino-sign red. Her chrome parts looked as if they were liquid. Her table and scoreboard pulsated. "Ooooh, the special is lit. Go for the special, cutie."

"You know, Ethyl, sweetheart," Wheeler confessed, "I think I'll always be jealous of those gleaming, original legs of yours."

He guided the ball into the lit special hole and in the nearly empty warehouse, Ethyl popped more loudly than ever before.

WIRED FOR MATE

"We're back with our next guest, Jasper Whitewall. Jasper is the current Wirechess champion of North America, here in San Francisco to defend his title. For the few of you who don't follow Wirechess, Jasper has been the champion for three years." The camera angle widened to include the man sitting beside the speaker. "Jasper, would you be so kind as to tell our viewing audience how Wirechess is played?"

"Certainly, Steve. As professional players, we have had our brains electronically altered so that we hallucinate in proportion to the level of play quality. If I'm playing a good game then I have good visions, which helps me concentrate and therefore my game improves. However," he said smugly, crossing his legs, "the opposite is true as well, and one wrong move can start a chain reaction of nightmarish hallucinations."

"Jasper, tonight your match is the opening game of the North American Wirechess Senior Tour. How do you feel you will fare?"

"Well, Steve, I have confidence that I will be representing the United States in the World Finals next fall. My opponent lacks the experience and intestinal fortitude necessary for the sport."

"So you are of the opinion that Wirechess is a sport?"

"Anyone who has ever played Wirechess at the pro level knows the risks involved, Steve. One can get seriously hurt. It's one thing to play amateur with the external jacks, but once you make the brain conversions, the game can be extremely brutal at times," Jasper said calmly.

"What about the claims that Wirechess is faked?" Steve asked.

"Look, if you don't believe the CAT scans, fine," replied the champion. "Look at Harvey Winchell's career. He left a trail of babbling idiots where geniuses once were, before he was banned from competition and disappeared. You think all those pros would fake insanity forever?"

"Assuming the damage is real, don't you think the possibility of being mentally injured should be lowered?"

"Steve, this is a game for the intellectual greats of our time. We know what we're getting into. If you took those possibilities away, there would be no way we could fill the Cow Palace tonight. People are out to see severe brain damage."

"Okay, we're getting low on time here." The host glanced at his teleprompter on the desk in front of him. "Jasper, you're going to be at the Cow Palace tonight, pitted against Lisa Rivera from the Dominican Republic. Where may our viewers outside the Bay Area see this?"

"It will be aired live on Pay-Per-View, and will be released on home video disc. Play-by-play commentary should be available on the seven major internetworks."

"Okay, thanks for coming." Steve turned to face another camera. "We'll be right back with a man who claims to be Elvis reincarnated."

After taping the *Up With Steve* segment, Jasper Whitewall had the taxi let him off at a small cafe. He had about two hours to kill until it was time to leave for the Cow Palace. He needed to sit and get his thoughts together before the match.

Rivera had induced a second personality in the previous Caribbean champion. It was the most horrid match he'd seen since watching Harvey Winchell as a teenager.

"I would like a double decaf mocha, please," Jasper said to the blond ponytailed person behind the counter who looked to be about seventeen. He was switching the music on the stereo, and didn't seem to notice.

"Hey, you got a customer up here," Jasper yelled.

"Well, stall him for me, will you? I'm busy," the ponytail muttered without looking around.

"Get up here and serve me, I haven't got all day."

The young man waited until he was done with the stereo and came up. "What did you want?"

"A double decaf mocha. I already told you," Jasper fumed.

"Look, don't make my life any more difficult than it needs to be by copping an attitude, okay?" he scolded motherly, going to work on the drink. The music kicked in. Jasper hated the music more than he despised the kid.

"What is this garbage? I don't think it's conducive to the dining atmosphere."

"First of all, the band's name is Ezra's Bad Habit. Secondly, this is a cafe, not a restaurant," he sneered, sliding the drink to him. "Two fifty."

"I don't like you. I can get you fired. I'm a very important man," Jasper threatened.

"I'll be careful. Now take your coffee and sit down."

Jasper was shocked. All he could do was give the guy his money and sit down. He took a table in the back and lit a cigarette. He thought about countering Rivera at her own game. She's too young, he thought, to have seen the master play. Harvey Winchell, you were the best. Well, second best. He snickered out loud and was reminiscing nicely when the smell of a litterbox interrupted him. He looked up to see a greasy, one-eyed wino standing there.

"Mr. Whitewall? Sorry to bother you, but my name is Mike, and I been a fan of yours for a long time now. I been real down and out, see, and lately I been real depressed. It's always been my dream to play you in chess. Whaddya say?" the man pleaded, sitting down and placing one of the cafe's chessboards on the table.

Jasper's ego had been rubbed, so he thought, Why not? and they set up and started to play. Jasper played white, moved a knight out, and the circuits in his brain started activating. The smell changed from litterbox to a pine forest. Jasper inhaled deeply. Mike followed with his move, looking intensely at the board.

Jasper moved his other knight and the music switched to Mozart. He moved a pawn and flowers sprouted from the floor. When he moved the bishop, the walls began to fade. Mike foolishly left a rook open which

Jasper took immediately, and the walls disappeared entirely and he was in a field with rabbits hopping about.

"Good thing you're not wired," Jasper grinned. Mike was wincing and pointing his finger at possibilities. The way he held his face looked familiar. "You remind me of someone. Someone famous, Jimi Hendrix? Nah, it'll come to me."

Mike made his move, taking one of Jasper's knights. Clouds started forming overhead, and something was wrong with his coffee. Mike had made either a brilliant move or a very lucky one. There was a possibility of trading four or five pieces to his advantage. The counter rematerialized from Jasper's hallucinations. The blond kid was still back there.

"Are you sure this is decaf?" Jasper whined. The kid looked over at Jasper, glared, and turned away. The counter disappeared. It was Jasper's move, and he was forced into taking one of Mike's bishops, but it left him vulnerable. The flowers sprouted thorns. A rabbit bit him on the foot.

Mike never looked up in the next five moves as he traded pieces with Jasper. He lost the same amount of pieces as Jasper, but attacked his king's side and ended with good positioning.

Jasper's world was crumbling. He knew a way out of this, but the rain was falling heavily and he couldn't concentrate with the rabbits chewing his feet, and the music was a wall of noise. All he could smell was sulfur. The chess pieces were incredibly hot, raindrops sizzling as they hit. His chair gave him splinters. He took a sip of his coffee and immediately spit out the murky bile.

"Aaaargh! Euyuck! What did you put in my drink?" Jasper yelled.

The blond-haired kid appeared suddenly, wearing a blood-splattered butcher's outfit with a huge knife in his right hand. "Look," he said, "if you can't keep all this yelling down, you're going to have to leave." With that, he faded away. Jasper heard snickering. He looked up into Mike's eye.

"What's the matter, Mr. Whitewall, something wrong?"

Suddenly, Mike looked just like Harvey Winchell. Jasper started to sweat. Even with the rain, he could feel his pores open up. He rubbed his eyes. This can't be Harvey Winchell, this must be a hallucination, he thought. Harvey's whereabouts are unknown, if this is him... Jasper knew he had to make the right move and fast. He couldn't concentrate well enough to remember the way out of this one, but there was always a way, wasn't there?

Jasper moved his remaining rook, which made the sulfur smell go away, but Mike countered by taking Jasper's queen. Stupid! Stupid! Stupid! Jasper thought, leaving her open like that! He stood up, the sulfur smell back and worse than before, and slammed his fists on the table. He looked down at his arms and saw maggots crawling from his skin. He felt the claws and teeth of evil rabbits crawling up his back, eating through to his spine. Harvey Winchell, it was Harvey Winchell! Only he could play like this, it couldn't be him, but it was... Jasper tried to walk away, but the thorny vines grabbed his ankles and he fell. The rabbits jumped all over his face and started ripping away his cheeks.

"Yeeearighjiggh," Jasper yelled, rolling on the floor.

"Whoa, cowboy," the counterperson's voice boomed. "That's all for you. Saddle up and head back to the ranch."

Jasper managed his way to his feet and looked at Mike, or Harvey Winchell, or whoever it was. He pointed a leprous finger at him.

"I don't know how you managed this," he moaned, "but you'd..." Jasper stopped. Mike's other eye came back, his clothes were new, and he had well-groomed hair. He looked exactly like Harvey Winchell, and he was laughing the Winchell laugh.

"The only way you can stop this is to finish the game, and from your present condition, you should probably start playing a little bit better," his opponent warned.

Play? Play what? Jasper thought, I'm just a humble leper. I just want to find a dry place away from the wild animals. I want a little food in my stomach. Jasper watched a seven-foot red devil with cloven hooves and a pitchfork walk his way. "You'll have to leave now," it said, lowering the fork.

Jasper ran from the counterperson into the street. Extremely malicious furry animals, stuck in his clothing, bit him repeatedly. His right leg broke off and he tripped on it, falling to the ground. He looked up. The last thing Jasper Whitewall ever saw was a herd of chrome fire-breathing buffalo headed straight for him.

manic d press
publications

King of the Roadkills. *Bucky Sinister.* $9.95

Alibi School. *Jeffrey McDaniel.* $8.95

The Underground Guide to San Francisco.
>   *edited by Jennifer Joseph.* $10.95

Signs of Life: channel-surfing through '90s culture.
>   *edited by Jennifer Joseph & Lisa Taplin.* $12.95

Beyond Definition: new writing from gay & lesbian san francisco.
>   *edited by Marci Blackman & Trebor Healey.* $10.95

Love Like Rage. *Wendy-o Matik* $7.00

The Language of Birds. *Kimi Sugioka* $7.00

The Rise and Fall of Third Leg. *Jon Longhi* $9.95

Specimen Tank. *Buzz Callaway* $10.95

The Verdict Is In.
>   *edited by Kathi Georges & Jennifer Joseph* $9.95

Elegy for the Old Stud. *David West* $7.00

The Back of a Spoon. *Jack Hirschman* $7.00

Mobius Stripper. *Bana Witt* $8.95

Baroque Outhouse / The Decapitated Head of a Dog.
>   *Randolph Nae* $7.00

Graveyard Golf and other stories. *Vampyre Mike Kassel* $7.95

Bricks and Anchors. *Jon Longhi* $8.00

The Devil Won't Let Me In. *Alice Olds-Ellingson* $7.95

Greatest Hits. *edited by Jennifer Joseph* $7.00

Lizards Again. *David Jewell* $7.00

The Future Isn't What It Used To Be. *Jennifer Joseph* $7.00

Acts of Submission. *Joie Cook* $4.00

Zucchini and other stories. *Jon Longhi* $3.00

Standing In Line. *Jerry D. Miley* $3.00

Drugs. *Jennifer Joseph* $3.00

Bums Eat Shit and other poems. *Sparrow 13* $3.00

Into The Outer World. *David Jewell* $3.00

Solitary Traveler. *Michele C.* $3.00

Night Is Colder Than Autumn. *Jerry D. Miley* $3.00

Seven Dollar Shoes. *Sparrow 13 LaughingWand.* $3.00

Intertwine. *Jennifer Joseph* $3.00

Feminine Resistance. *Carol Cavileer* $3.00

Now Hear This. *Lisa Radon.* $3.00

Bodies of Work. *Nancy Depper* $3.00

Corazon Del Barrio. *Jorge Argueta.* $4.00

Please add $2.00 to all orders for postage and handling.

manic d press
box 410804
san francisco ca 94141 usa

distributed to the trade by publishers group west